D0877098

HIS HOMETOWN GIRL

CINDY KIRK

WAVERLY
HOUSE

Copyright © 2022 by Cynthia Rutledge

All rights reserved

No part of this book may be reproduced in any form or by any electronic or mechanical means, including information storage and retrieval systems, without written permission from the author, except for the use of brief quotations in a book review.

This is a work of fiction. Names, characters, places and incidents are products of the author's imagination or are used fictitiously. Any resemblance to actual events, locales, organizations, or persons, living or dead, is entirely coincidental.

ISBN: 9798815979314

First published in 2013 as HIS VALENTINE BRIDE by Silhouette Books

CHAPTER ONE

Elizabeth "Betsy" McGregor had been out of work for six weeks, three days and twelve hours. With Thanksgiving closing in, Betsy knew if she didn't get a job before the holiday season began, she might as well forget about finding one until after the first of the year. Her desperate straits had smacked her in the face last weekend when she'd put pen to paper and determined she only had enough money for one more rent payment. That was the *only* reason she'd agreed to interview for a position with Ryan Harcourt's law firm.

Okay, perhaps the medallion she'd dropped into the pocket of her suit jacket this morning had something to do with her decision. She'd been trying to decide if she should keep the interview or cancel when she found the octagon-shaped copper coin while cleaning out her Great Aunt's home. After reading the accompanying note her recently deceased aunt had addressed to her, Betsy had been seized with a certainty that her luck was about to change.

No matter that the percentage of unemployed in Jackson Hole was on the rise or that the holidays were just around the corner.

According to Aunt Agatha, the medallion would bring her not only good luck, but love.

She snorted. It would take a lot for a tarnished metal coin engraved with ivy, a few hearts and some funny French words to send love her way. Luck, she could believe. But love?

Betsy had never been one to lie to herself. Not only was she rapidly approaching thirty, she was the epitome of the word *average*. Average height. Average weight. Average looks. Even her hair was average. Instead of being a rich chestnut brown like her best friend, Adrianna Lee, the strands hanging down her back were a mousy shade of tan. It figured that her eyes couldn't be a vivid emerald green—like Adrianna's—but instead were a dusty blue. Not light enough to be interesting nor dark enough to be striking.

Her features were arranged nicely enough, although if she could wave a magic wand, the sprinkle of freckles across the bridge of her nose would be banished forever. The only good thing Betsy could say about her appearance was that she was so ordinary she could blend in anywhere.

She pulled the key from the ignition, accepting the truth but irritated by it nonetheless. She didn't want to be ordinary. Or to blend in. Just once she'd like to be the type of woman who turned heads when she walked down the street. The type of woman a man would see and immediately want by his side. The type of woman a man like Ryan Harcourt could love.

Heat flooded her face at the realization that she was still as foolish as she'd been at age ten when she'd secretly vowed to marry the slender dark-haired boy with the slate grey eyes.

It hadn't mattered that he was five years older or that all the middle school girls drooled over him. Unlike most of her brother's friends, Ryan had always been nice to her. She vividly remembered the day he'd come across some boys taunting her, saying horrible things and making her cry. Ryan had not only run them off, he'd walked her home. That was the day she'd fallen in love with him.

That's why working for him made absolutely no sense. Seeing him every day would be a dream come true and her worst nightmare. He'd be nice to her. She didn't doubt that in the least. But to have someone see you as only an employee when you yearned for him to see you as a desirable woman, well, it was bound to be difficult.

Still, she'd had a lot of experience handling challenging situations. Hadn't she survived a childhood with an alcoholic mother and an absent father? The bottom line was she needed a job. She had to have money to pay her bills and to replace the red-tagged furnace at the house she'd inherited from her aunt.

While she hoped the medallion in her pocket would bring good fortune, she wasn't counting on it. That would be foolhardy. Betsy had always been a firm believer that God helped those who helped themselves. That's just what she was doing by interviewing for this job; tossing a Hail Mary and hoping for a touchdown.

Squaring her shoulders Betsy stepped from her parked car then paused at the curb to straighten the cuffs of her best camel-colored suit. Since the temperature was a balmy forty-two degrees, she'd slipped on a tan all-weather coat instead of her thick fur-lined parka, the one her brother said made her look like an Eskimo.

The snow from the small storm two days ago had already begun to melt, turning the streets into a slushy mess. Yet the sky was a vivid blue and Betsy reveled in the feel of the sun on her face.

She let her coat hang open and started down the sidewalk toward Ryan's office. Though she tried to walk slowly, all too soon the frontage for his office came into view. She glanced at her watch and grimaced. Arriving ten minutes prior to an interview was appropriate. Twenty minutes early smacked of desperation.

While she might indeed be desperate, Betsy certainly didn't want to give that impression. Perhaps it'd be best if she relaxed in her car a little while longer.

She abruptly turned back in the direction of her vehicle, her mind consumed with the upcoming interview until her heel caught in a crack, plunging her forward.

A tiny cry sprang from her throat as the sidewalk rushed up to greet her. At the last second, a man behind her reached out and grabbed her.

His hands were strong, pulling her to him, steadying her. The chest he held her against was broad. She lifted her head, the words of sincere thanks already formed on her lips. Then she saw his face. Suddenly Betsy found it difficult to think, much less speak. She finally found her voice. "Ryan?"

He smiled. That boyish, slightly crooked grin guaranteed to make a woman's heart skip a beat. It was hard to imagine she'd been in Jackson Hole all these months without their paths crossing. That wasn't completely accurate. A week or so ago she'd seen him at a local sports bar but he'd been too busy chatting with friends to notice her.

Even from a distance, it had been apparent the years had been good to him. Despite being a regular on the rodeo circuit during his college days, Ryan was one of those guys who only got better with age. He was slender, just as she remembered, but now with a man's broad shoulders and lean hips. His dark hair brushed his collar and tiny laugh lines edged his eyes.

She let her gaze linger a second longer on the crush-of-her-youth packaged in grey dress pants, a charcoal-colored shirt and dark topcoat. After a moment all she could see were those beautiful silver eyes that a girl, er woman, could get lost in...

"Betsy?" Her name sounded like a husky caress on his lips.

She shivered but not from the cold. In fact, she felt positively warm. Okay, hot. His arms remained around her. Betsy couldn't remember the last time she'd been this close to him. It felt...nice.

"Are you okay?" His beautiful eyes were filled with concern.

She managed a nod and the lines of worry between his brows eased.

"I was on my way to the office," he said. "I saw your name on the interview list and didn't want to keep you waiting."

Though prior to running into him she'd barely walked ten feet, her breath now came in short puffs. Every inch of her body sizzled.

"Until I received your application, I didn't know you'd moved back." As if realizing he still held her in his arms he stepped back and let his arms drop to his side.

Betsy resisted the urge to pull him back close. Instead, she forced a smile. "I've been here almost three months. I was working at Dunlop and Sons but they cut back on employees."

She saw no reason to mention that Chad Dunlop had wanted to fire her. Only some quick thinking and determination on her part had kept her work reputation intact.

Ryan tilted his head, confusion furrowing his brow. "Hearing that firm is downsizing surprises me. I thought they'd be adding personnel, not cutting back."

Betsy let a slight shrug be her response.

"Tell me about your work in Kansas City." He took her arm and they continued down the street in the direction of his office.

Despite the layers of clothing between them, Betsy's arm tingled beneath his touch. She found herself slowing her steps, wishing his office wasn't so close. She'd like to prolong this time for a few minutes more. It seemed like they'd barely started walking when they reached the glass storefront of his law practice.

To her surprise, Ryan kept walking.

She glanced back over her shoulder. "Wasn't that your office?"

"Why don't we do the interview at Hill of Beans?" He opened

the wooden door, stepping aside and waving her inside. "After your altercation with the sidewalk, I'm sure you need a hot chocolate or a latte to steady your nerves."

"That works." Betsy fought back a rush of pleasure. Going to Jackson's newest coffee shop with Ryan made this feel more like a date than an interview.

For a Tuesday, the coffee shop--known for its fabulous selection of beverages and bakery items--was surprisingly busy. Although Betsy insisted she wasn't hungry, Ryan got a large piece of coffee cake for them to share as well as two cups of hot cocoa.

Once they were settled in a booth by the window, Betsy expected him to start rattling off questions. She'd been through so many interviews in the past couple of months she doubted there was anything he could ask that would catch her off-guard.

"I was sorry to hear about your mom."

Okay, he'd surprised her. Betsy couldn't remember the last time anyone had mentioned her mother. When she was small, everyone was always commenting on the resemblance. Back then Betsy had been proud to be compared to her beautiful mother.

It wasn't until she got a little older that she realized her mother wasn't pretty. Not on the outside and certainly not on the inside.

"She was drunk when she hit the telephone pole," Betsy said in the unemotional tone she'd cultivated over the years. "The police said she was going seventy. She barely missed a kid on a bike."

"She was your mother," he said softly. "Her death had to hurt."

Betsy didn't say anything.

"Is that why you moved back to Jackson?" His large hands encircled the tan coffee mug. "To settle her estate?"

"What estate?" Betsy gave a little laugh. "All she left was a bunch of bills."

She wondered what Ryan would think if she told him the reason she'd stayed in KC until now was because she'd refused to move back to Jackson Hole as long as her mother was here? He *should* understand. After all, as Keenan's friend he'd witnessed Gloria's out-of-control drunken rages.

"I'd wanted to move back for some time," Betsy said in a matter-of-fact tone. "Adrianna Lee has been encouraging me to 'return to my roots' for years."

Ryan's eyes took on a gleam she couldn't quite decipher. "That's right. I'd forgotten you and Adrianna were good friends."

"Since kindergarten." A smile lifted Betsy's lips, the way it always did when she thought of her oldest and dearest friend.

"I've seen her at Wally's Place," he said, referring to the popular sports bar that was at the top of everyone's list. "Rarely with the same guy twice."

"I guess she just hasn't found Mr. Right." Betsy kept her tone light. While Adrianna was beautiful and bright with a great job as an OB-GYN nurse midwife, her friend had her own demons that made it difficult to trust men.

"Enough about her." Ryan waved a dismissive hand. "Let's talk about you. How did you like Kansas City?"

His gaze settled on Betsy, as if she was the only woman in the world. Or, at least, the only one who mattered. Though it was a heady feeling to be the object of such focus, she knew this was simply Ryan's way. The guy was a natural born charmer and she'd do well to keep that fact front and center in her head.

"I liked Kansas, but Wyoming has always been home."

"Your resume said you graduated from KU with a degree in Political Science." He smiled and a teasing glint filled his eyes. "Looks like you were planning to go to law school. Am I right?"

"I considered it," Betsy admitted. "But I really love being a paralegal."

Betsy went on to tell Ryan that after high school, she'd moved to Lawrence to live with a cousin. She'd worked for a year as a waitress then decided to give higher education a shot. "After graduating from KU I moved to Kansas City and completed a paralegal program in Overland Park."

"I bet you're a dynamite legal assistant," he said with such sincerity that tears stung the back of her eyes.

"My past employers all seemed to think so." With the exception of Chad Dunlop, of course.

"Now you're back in Jackson Hole to stay."

Betsy nodded. "Shortly after my mother died, my great-aunt passed away and left me her house. Once the furnace is repaired and the city says it's safe for me to occupy, I'll move in."

"The place sounds like a real gem."

Another woman might have taken offense, but Betsy simply laughed. "It's definitely a fixer-upper, that's for sure."

Having a place to stay rent-free—at least once she could move in—was a big plus. But to survive in Jackson Hole, Betsy needed a job. Lately she'd considered practicing saying 'do you want fries with that?' but she enjoyed being a legal assistant and was darn good at her job. Before she gave up on the hope of getting a position in her field, she had to know she'd left no stone unturned.

"You got a great recommendation from the Kansas firm." Ryan offered an encouraging smile. "Tell me about your duties there."

"They were a large, diverse practice. Initially I worked for one of the older partners who primarily practiced family law. He had a stroke and was out of the office for an extended period. During that time I helped several of the other partners, which gave me a wide range of experiences."

Betsy went on to describe her duties in greater depths. There were so many interesting stories that she continued to talk. She was halfway through the third example when she realized he was smiling at her.

She stopped and raised a hand to her face, praying she didn't have a hot cocoa mustache or something equally horrifying. "Do I have something on my face? In my teeth?"

"No. Why?"

"You were looking at me so strangely."

He cocked his head. "Was I?"

"You know you were." If this was a regular interview, she'd never have challenged him. But this was Ryan.

"I'm just impressed by the breadth of your experience."

Was that honest-to-goodness admiration she saw reflected in those gorgeous eyes? Before she could respond, a gruff voice filled the air.

"Who let you in the front door?"

Betsy looked up into the grinning face of Cole Lassiter. The owner of the Hill of Beans coffee empire and another of Ryan's many friends from high school, had a devilish gleam in his eyes.

"Don't think I didn't notice the timing, Lassiter," Ryan shot back. "You wait until I pay and *then* you show up."

Cole chuckled, grabbed a chair from a nearby table and sat down at the edge of the booth. He gave Betsy a curious glance. Since moving back, she'd seen Cole, his wife Margaret and son Charlie in church, but only from a distance.

He was a handsome man with thick dark hair and vivid blue eyes. He and Ryan look a lot alike, so much so that back in high school, those who didn't know them well would often mistake one for the other.

"Aren't you going to introduce me?" Cole's gaze lingered on Betsy.

"Are you blind?" The look on Ryan's face would have been laughable at any other time. "It's Betsy McGregor, Keenan's little sister."

Cole shook his head and gave a low whistle. "You were a girl the last time I saw you. Now look at you, all grown up and beautiful."

Was that a scowl on Ryan's face? Betsy simply laughed. All her brother's friends had been blessed with an abundance of charm.

"Congratulations on marrying Margaret Fisher," Betsy said. "I knew her younger sister better than I did her, but Margaret was always nice to me when I stopped over."

"I'm a lucky man." The look on Cole's face told her he meant every word.

"She might not remember me but be sure and tell her I said hello."

"Oh, she'll remember," Cole said gallantly. His gaze shifted from Ryan to her then back to Ryan again. "Are you...dating?"

"Goodness, no." Betsy spoke quickly before Ryan had a chance to respond. Or heaven forbid, *laugh*. "I'm interviewing to be his legal assistant."

Cole shifted his gaze to Ryan. "What happened to Caroline?"

"Her husband got a promotion. They're leaving for Texas tomorrow."

"Good for them," Cole said pointedly. "Bad for you."

"I was bummed. Until I received Betsy's application." Ryan shifted his gaze to her and smiled. "The job is yours, if you want it."

"Just like that?" Betsy's voice rose. "Aren't you going to check my references?"

He leaned forward resting his arms on the table. "Just tell me you don't have any deep dark secrets, we're good."

CHAPTER TWO

When Friday night rolled around, Ryan had his evening planned. Meet some friends at Wally's Place, toss back a few cold ones and play a game or two of darts. Then he overheard Betsy talking on the phone to Adrianna and learned there was a party at Michelle Kerns' house that evening.

Ryan knew the young OB-GYN but not well enough to merit an invitation to her home. When he heard Adrianna was going to be there, his plans for the evening did a one-eighty. Somehow, some way, he would find a way to attend that party.

He made a few calls and within a matter of minutes, Mitzi Sanchez reluctantly agreed he could go with her. Mitzi was an orthopedic surgeon he'd dated a few times. As much as he enjoyed Mitzi's company, the chemistry wasn't there. Now they were simply good friends. Okay, that might be stretching it a bit.

Still, they were good enough friends that he could tag along with her. Mitzi had made it clear that once they got to the party, he was on his own.

"Would you quit primping," Mitzi said in a teasing tone as they made their way up the walk to Michelle's townhome. "I swear you're worse than any girl."

He finished adjusting the cuffs of his sweater. "I love you, too." She rolled her eyes.

"Seriously, thanks for making me your plus-one tonight." He glanced down at his black jeans and cowboy boots. While the sweater under his jacket dressed up his party attire, he hoped he hadn't gone too casual. Adrianna was a hard woman to impress and he'd already blown several opportunities.

"You're not my plus-one," she said. "I just didn't have the sense to say no."

That's what Ryan liked about Mitzi. She told it as she saw it. It was a shame there was no chemistry between them, because not only was she a beautiful woman, she could sing karaoke like a pro.

"I don't know you," he said as they reached the stoop. "Once you get me through the front door, that is."

"You'll owe me, Harcourt." She brushed back a strand of brown hair that looked as if it had been streaked with peanut butter.

"The first time you get slapped with a malpractice suit, I'm your man."

"What a pleasant thought." She reached out to press the doorbell, but he gently pushed her arm down.

"Allow me."

"Such a gentleman."

"I aim to please," he shot her a wink just as the door opened.

Before she could object, Ryan placed an arm loosely around her shoulders. He half-expected Mitzi to shrug it off or punch him in the side, instead she gave a long-suffering sigh. "Michelle, I believe you know Ryan Harcourt."

"Of course." The hostess clasped his hand firmly in greeting. She was tall, with honey colored hair and big blue eyes. "Welcome. We have wine and beer and snacks. Help yourself to whatever you want."

For a second, Ryan's gaze drifted to where Adrianna stood.

He felt Mitzi's eyes on him as he placed his coat in Michelle's outstretched hand. For an uncanny moment he had the feeling he could read her mind.

"The answer is no," Mitzi said as the hostess stepped away, leaving them alone.

"You don't even know the question," he protested.

"I have my suspicions."

"Ryan," a familiar voice behind him gasped. "Why didn't you mention you were coming tonight?"

He turned to see Betsy standing in the hallway near what was obviously the kitchen, holding a glass of white wine. Like the hostess and most of the other women in the room, she wore jeans and a sweater suitable for the ski slopes.

She'd done something different with her hair. He narrowed his gaze. "You look nice."

"You like it?" Pleasure ran through her words. She raised a hand to her hair that had been long and sleek during the day but now stopped at her shoulders and had a bunch of layers. "I got it cut after work."

The new style emphasized her large eyes and made her cheekbones more pronounced. He realized suddenly that his friend's sister—and his new employee--was a very attractive woman. "I do like it."

Even if he hadn't, the blinding smile she shot him would have been worth any lie. But it was the truth and he was glad he'd said it.

"Are you and Mitzi dating?" she asked, twisting the toe of her shoe into the hardwood.

Ryan glanced across the room where his "date" stood chatting with Benedict Campbell, one of the physicians in her practice. Though Mitzi claimed to hate the man, she'd protested so much that Ryan suspected there were some red-hot sparks beneath that animosity.

"Nah," he said. "She just didn't want to come to the party alone so I agreed to come with her."

He glanced around the room. Smooth jazz was playing low in the background and the wine was being served in crystal glasses. Although everyone was dressed casually—practically a given in Jackson Hole—Ryan instantly knew that this wasn't his kind of party. Although he'd gone back east for law school and had attended many elegant events, he was a country boy at heart. Give him a can of beer, a bowl of chips and football on the flat screen and he was happy.

"Who did you come with?" he asked Betsy politely. Not because he was particularly interested in who she was dating but rather to pass the time while he searched the room for the woman he'd come to see.

"Oh look, there's Adrianna," Betsy said.

Like a hunting dog that had just gotten a whiff of a delectable scent, Ryan stiffened. He forced a casual smile to his lips. "I haven't seen Adrianna in months. I bet I wouldn't even recognize her."

Even as he said the words, Ryan had to stifle a smile. As if he'd ever forget even the minutest detail about anything to do with Adrianna.

"Oh, I'm sure you would," Betsy said with great earnestness. "She looks the same. The stylist tried to get her to try something different but you know Adrianna. She dug in those heels and refused to let him touch her hair."

"Her hair is beautiful," Ryan said without thinking. "It would have been a shame to cut it."

"Ryan agrees with you," he heard Betsy say and shifted his gaze to see who she was speaking with.

"Really." Adrianna's cool green eyes settled on him. "About what?"

"About cutting your hair," Betsy said, seemingly oblivious to the sudden tension in the air. "He said why fool with perfection?"

Ryan didn't remember saying those exact words but it was a true sentiment, nonetheless.

Adrianna didn't appear impressed. In fact, she was looking at him as if he was the lowest form of worm. Surely, she wasn't holding that one little prank all those years ago against him?

"Ryan is the best boss, Anna," Betsy said, the words laden with sincerity. "I'm so glad I returned to Jackson Hole."

"I'm certainly happy you're back, Bets." A warmth filled Adrianna's voice and, when she glanced at Ryan, some of the coolness in her eyes thawed. The nurse midwife appeared to appreciate him more because he'd been good to her friend.

Ryan wondered if telling Adrianna that he'd given Betsy the afternoon off would give him extra points or make him look like a suck up. He decided not to chance it. "I couldn't believe it when Betsy showed up to interview but I'm sure glad she did."

From the continued thawing in Adrianna's eyes, he was on to something here.

"Can I get you something to drink?" he asked, smiling at her. He would have included Betsy, but she already had a drink in her hand.

"I'm good." Instead of meeting his gaze and letting him drown in those emerald green depths, she glanced around the room. "There's Travis and Mary Karen Fisher. I need to pop over and say hello."

Ryan's heart dropped as she started to walk away, her high heeled boots clicking on the hardwood. At the last minute, she glanced over her shoulder and flashed him a brilliant smile.

"You take care of Betsy," she said, in a low husky voice. "See that she has a good time."

"Anna," Betsy moaned, but Ryan scarcely noticed.

How long had it been since Adrianna had smiled at him with such warmth? Years, he thought to himself, too many to count.

∾

Betsy stared at her friend's retreating back and felt heat rise up her neck. The next time she got Adrianna alone, she was going to read her the riot act. Why she'd practically thrown her at Ryan.

Not that he'd protested, she thought, looking for the silver lining. He seemed in a remarkably good mood.

"Do you want to scope out the appetizers?" she asked. "Not that you have to go with me. Adrianna was just kidding. I don't need anyone taking care of me."

She was on the verge of saying more when she snapped her mouth shut. When she got nervous, she had a tendency to babble and right now she was poised to babble with the best of them.

"I'd like to check out the food." He held out his arm. "If I remember correctly the only thing you need to avoid is anything with shrimp."

Betsy groaned. Honest to goodness groaned. "Of all the things to remember, you had to recall that?"

"It's not every day I got to see a person covered in hives," he said with a little too much enthusiasm for her liking. "You even had them in your—"

"—hair," she said. "Yes, I remember."

"Keenan put that pink stuff all over your skin," he said warming to the memory. "It looked like Pepto Bismol."

"Don't remind me." She remembered that night well. Her mother had been out running around God knows where and Betsy had been hungry. She'd eaten some old shrimp rollups they'd had in the freezer. That's when the hives had broken out. She'd been terrified, then relieved when Keenan had come home early.

But when she saw who he was with, her terror had turned to horror. The last person she wanted to see her with those big red welts covering her skin was Ryan. She remembered he hadn't laughed or made fun of her. He's simply called his parents to find out what they should do.

While Keenan had helped smear the Caladryl lotion on her

hard-to-reach places, Ryan had run to the corner store and gotten an antihistamine for her to take. By the time her mother finally dragged herself through the front door at three am, the hives had already started to fade.

"Hey." He leaned closer, a teasing glint in his eyes. "How many men can say they've seen you covered in hives?"

"Har, har." Betsy was thankful her voice came out all casual and offhand. Which was a real feat considering her knees had gone boneless and she was having difficulty thinking with him so close.

He sat back and his gaze zeroed in on a large buffet table at the back of the great room. A pristine white linen cloth with scalloped edges covered the oak top but it appeared to be the food which had captured Ryan's attention.

"Is that a shrimp cocktail?" He turned to her, his eyes wide and guileless. "I could get you one. Maybe you're not allergic anymore."

Betsy jabbed him in the ribs, forgetting he was the man she'd loved for years. "Settle down. Or I'm going to tell everyone the story of when Keenan locked you out of the locker room in your boxers--"

"You're right. Stay clear of the shrimp."

She couldn't help it. Betsy laughed with sheer joy. This was the Ryan she wanted. Not the perfectly behaved boss who hadn't cracked one joke all week, but the Ryan who made her laugh and with whom she shared a common history.

If only she could figure out a way to capture this moment. Better yet, find a way to translate friendship into love.

In the past ninety minutes Adrianna had talked to everyone but him. Ryan wasn't discouraged. He'd already accomplished a lot for one evening. When the hostess suggested a rousing game of charades, he knew it was time to leave on a high note.

Ryan glanced at the woman by his side, delicately picking a piece of chicken meat from the bone. Her brows were pulled together and she was studying the tiny piece of meat as if it was a complex legal case she was researching. He got the feeling Betsy was bored, too.

He had to admit she was what had saved this party from being a total wash-out. They'd roamed the room like a couple of old friends, laughing and talking to others they knew and some they'd just met. The buffet table had drawn their attention several times and they'd picked and chosen from its sumptuous bounty.

Betsy was fun, with a quick wit and a sly sense of humor in sync with his own. They talked about the old days and he'd just finished reliving his high school prom debacle when Betsy had decided she desperately needed a few more wings.

"It's no wonder you had to lasso a few more," he said to her. "There isn't enough meat on one to feed an ant."

A becoming shade of pink rose up her neck but she lifted her chin. "I didn't eat supper. I'm not quite the porker I appear to be."

"Porker?" He dropped his gaze and slowly surveyed her lean figure. "Not hardly."

The pink on her cheeks deepened to red.

"You don't need to make nice," she said with a dismissive wave. "I love to eat. Several times during my childhood I was sorely tempted to cut the candy heart out of my Raggedy Ann."

"You played with dolls?"

"I did when I was a little girl."

"You just never seemed the doll playing type to me," he said. "I don't recall seeing any lying around your house."

"That's because I didn't have any." Betsy dropped the chicken wing to her plate then wiped her fingers on a linen napkin. "Not until Keenan brought Raggedy Ann for me with his paper route money. She was my first and only doll. He was ten and I was five."

"Keenan bought a doll with his paper route money." Ryan could barely fathom that the rough and tumble friend from his youth would do something like that, even if it was for his little sister.

The realization that perhaps he hadn't known Keenan as well as he thought he did hadn't even had time to settle in when Betsy grabbed the front of his sweater in her hand and pulled him close. "Don't you say one word to him about it, either." Her eyes grew piercing. "Understand?"

Ryan considered teasing her a bit more, but something in her eyes made him simply nod. Growing up in the McGregor household hadn't been easy for either Keenan or Betsy. The fact that his friend had found a way to make life easier on his little sister had Ryan respecting Keenan even more.

Betsy's gaze drifted to the groups already forming for the game. She wrinkled her nose. "I hate charades."

"That makes two of us," Ryan said. "Want to sneak out?"

A look he couldn't quite decipher skittered across Betsy's face. Then she sighed. "You came with Mitzi, remember?"

Mitzi? Heck, he hadn't seen the brunette since he'd walked through the door behind her. That was just the way they both wanted it. "We drove separately."

Ryan thought for a minute. He hadn't seen Betsy with anyone all night, with the exception of him, of course. That didn't mean she hadn't come with someone. "What about you?"

"I'm on my own." The words came out on a little sigh.

"Good."

She cocked her head. "Why good?"

He smiled. "Because you and I are going to do some serious partying and now there's nothing standing in our way."

CHAPTER THREE

Betsy glanced at the glass of wine in her hand. Had someone slipped something in her drink? That was the only explanation. She had to be hallucinating. There was no way on God's green earth that Ryan Harcourt would ask *her* to party with him.

She glanced up and into those eyes that reminded her of liquid silver. "Pardon?"

"Good. I knew you'd be up for it." He disappeared into a bedroom and returned with two coats, her Eskimo-inspired parka and his stylish, but rugged, LL Bean coat.

"How'd you know this one was mine?" she asked, slipping her arm into one sleeve.

"You've worn it to the office every day this week."

Yes, but it had also been safely tucked into the coat closet by the time he arrived. While it was warm, Betsy was well aware it wasn't the most fashionable of outerwear. It was now obvious that all her stealth had been for nothing.

The man was observant. Too observant. Alarm bells began ringing in her head. He'd noticed her coat. What would be next? Would he one day look in her eyes and see what she tried so hard to hide?

He can't know that I love him. I won't allow that to happen.

"Nothing gets past you," she said with a half-hearted chuckle.

"Thanks for the compliment," he said, sounding pleased.

Before Betsy knew what was happening, he'd hauled her off to the hostess, they'd said their good-byes to everyone, including Adrianna who seemed oddly pleased to see her best friend leaving the party early.

Since Betsy and Ryan both lived not far from downtown Jackson, she dropped her car at her home and they took his truck from there. She wasn't sure it was a good idea. What if she wanted to leave the bar before Ryan was ready to go? He assured her that he would leave whenever she said the word.

She supposed it made sense to ride together. After all, parking was at a premium in downtown Jackson, especially on a weekend night. Luckily a big Ram 4X4 was just pulling out of a spot on the street when they drew close.

Ryan shot a smile at her and stopped to wait. "Looks like this is our lucky day."

Our lucky day. Not his lucky day. Not her lucky day. But *ours*.

Though Betsy liked the sound of that, liked it a lot, it didn't mean she'd lost all power of rational thought. She knew she'd simply been in the right place at the right time. Ryan had wanted to ditch the party and it looked better to be leaving with her than to leave alone. Still 'our lucky day' did have a nice ring.

"I'm going to leave my coat in the car," Betsy said as he pulled into the vacated parking spot. She unfastened her seatbelt then reached for the zipper to her parka.

"Let me help you with that." Ryan leaned over and assisted her with slipping the jacket from her shoulders.

She looked up and their eyes met. Electricity filled the air. Betsy held her breath.

When he stepped from the truck without saying another word, she decided it must have been only her own overactive imagination conjuring up something that wasn't there.

"I'm glad we found a close spot." Betsy said over her shoulder. She'd started hurrying along the sidewalk the second her boots hit the pavement. Though she knew it would be toasty warm inside the crowded bar, outside the wind held a bone chilling bite.

Despite her rush, Ryan still reached the door to the bar first. Like a proper gentleman, he pulled it open then stepped aside, motioning her inside.

Betsy slipped past him, taking one deep breath of his spicy cologne before the pleasing scent was lost in the smell of sawdust, French fried potatoes and peanuts.

Ryan leaned close, shouting in her ear. "It's packed tonight."

She nodded, unable to keep the smile from her face. She couldn't remember the last time she'd been so happy. Okay, it had been last week when Ryan had told her the job was hers. And again, that day, when she'd learned that the salary was considerably higher than what she'd been making at her previous position.

This, well, this was different. This was a fantasy come to life. A night out with Ryan. She felt as if she was at a Craps table in Vegas rolling sevens.

"Ryan, ohmigod, someone said you weren't coming tonight."

The sexy, breathless voice belonged to one of the blondes Betsy had seen him with last week. Her hair was tousled around her pretty face, but it wasn't her bright smile that seemed to capture Ryan's attention. It was her chambray shirt with pearl buttons hanging open, showing an amazing amount of cleavage. Even Betsy was impressed.

Snake eyes, she could almost hear the Craps dealer call out. Her luck had come to an end.

"Who's she?" The young blonde's brows furrowed as she finally noticed the former bull-rider wasn't alone.

"This is Betsy," Ryan crooked a companionable arm around her shoulders. "She's an old friend."

Old friend. Hmmm. Better than saying she was his employee.

The blonde looked her up and down, clearly not liking where Ryan's arm was positioned. "I bet you don't play darts."

Before Betsy could answer, the woman jerked a thumb toward Ryan. "Me and him are a winning combination."

"I've tossed quite a few in my time." *Quite a few* may have been a bit of an exaggeration but Keenan had taught her how to hold and toss a dart. At one time she'd been pretty good at it, too. That had been years ago.

"I don't think so," the girl sniffed.

Betsy felt the hair on the back of her neck stand up. She narrowed her gaze. "Are you calling me a liar?"

"Ladies, ladies." Ryan may have spoken to both of them but it was Betsy who found herself on the end of his conciliatory smile. "There's no shame in not playing."

He thought she was lying, too. Betsy pressed her lips together and counted to ten. When she finally found her voice, she pinned the young blonde with her gaze. "Let's play a game. Then you can offer me an apology."

A momentary indecision filled the girl's gaze. She shot a glance in Ryan's direction.

Someone handed him a beer and he smiled benignly at the two women. "Sounds like a good solution to me," he said, taking a sip.

Suspicion filled the blonde's eyes. She glanced from Ryan to Betsy. "Is this some kind of set-up?"

"A set-up?" Betsy asked, puzzled.

Ryan simply grinned and took another drink.

"It is." The blonde tossed her head, sending her hair cascading down her back. "Well, you can forget it. I'm not playing along."

She turned abruptly and sashayed her way across the bar, her head held high.

"What's up with her?" Betsy asked.

"Heidi doesn't—"

"Her name is Heidi?" Betsy bit back a giggle, the name conjuring up an image of a mountain girl frolicking with goats.

Ryan began to nod, then paused. "At least I *think* that's her name."

"She looks more like a Bambi to me." The second the words left her mouth, Betsy wished she could pull them back. Though the girl's attitude rubbed her wrong, there was no need to stoop to her level.

"Maybe that is her name," Ryan said, her comment appearing to have gone straight over his head. "I don't remember."

The fact that he wasn't really on a first name basis with the curvaceous blonde buoyed Betsy's spirits. She couldn't keep a smile from her lips.

"Can I get you something to drink?" he asked.

"Club soda with a twist of lime, please."

"Ah, so you've decided to be a little wild and crazy tonight," he said teasingly. "I like it."

He'd barely left for the bar when Betsy saw her former employer, Chad Dunlop, making his way through the crowd. Dressed in jeans and a navy long-sleeved cotton shirt, he looked different than he did in the office. There he always wore a hand-tailored suit and shiny Italian shoes with names she couldn't begin to pronounce.

She supposed she could have moved, or looked away, but she didn't. When she'd walked out of his family's law offices all those weeks ago, Betsy had vowed that she wouldn't let anyone make her feel like a victim. If anyone should feel awkward about their paths crossing again, it should be him.

He saw her and changed course, making his trajectory one that would intersect with her. It figured that he wasn't smart enough to leave well enough alone.

Betsy wasn't sure of his motives, but there was one thing of which she was certain. She wasn't going to run or back down. If

Chad was foolish enough to cause a scene, the only loser tonight was going to be him.

While Ryan waited at the bar for Betsy's club soda—with a hint of lime—he chatted with a few of the wait staff. Out of the corner of one eye, he kept an eye on Betsy. Although he'd expected her to snag a table, she stood in the same spot he'd left her.

The only difference was her back was now ramrod straight. As he watched, she lifted her chin.

"Hurry up, Wally," he said to the bartender without moving his gaze from Betsy. "The lady is really thirsty."

It wasn't true, but Betsy was Keenan's little sister and nothing was going to happen to her on Ryan's watch. For some reason, he had a feeling she needed him.

"Here you go." The plump, bald-headed owner of the establishment set the drink on the bar. "Can I get you a draw?"

"Not now." Without shifting his gaze from Betsy, Ryan curved his fingers around her glass of soda.

He started through the crowd, smiling when someone called out a greeting or slapped him on the shoulder but not slowing his steps. Ryan was almost to Betsy when he saw him.

Chad Dunlop had been a senior at Jackson Hole high school when Ryan was a sophomore. They'd been on the football team at the same time. Ryan had no use for the man. As a boy, he'd had a mean streak. As a man, there was something about him Ryan didn't trust.

From the defiant way she was standing, Betsy didn't like the guy any more than he did. Though Chad had given her a glowing letter of recommendation, Ryan wondered if there was more to the story of her departure than a simple downsizing.

No time like the present to find out. He reached his friend's little sister at the same time as the attorney.

"Chad," Ryan said in a hearty tone. "Didn't expect to see you here tonight."

Ryan turned to Betsy and handed her the club soda. "Sorry it took so long."

Chad's gaze turned sharp and assessing. "You're together?"

"Betsy and I are old friends," Ryan said. "I understand she worked for you for a while."

For a second, the man's smooth façade slipped and the bully Ryan remembered from all those years ago, stood before him.

"Yeah, what of it? We had to downsize." Chad's pale blue eyes settled on Betsy. "Whatever else she told you is a lie."

Anger rolled off Betsy in waves. If looks could kill, Chad would be six feet under.

"She didn't tell me anything." Ryan kept his gaze fixed on the tall blonde man. "It sounds as if there's something to tell."

Chad shot Betsy a warning glance then turned to Ryan. "Lynnette is waiting for me at home. We're taking the kids over to the grandparents tonight."

If Chad was trying to convince Ryan he was a committed family man, he might as well have saved his breath. Ryan had seen the way the guy flirted with the wait staff.

"Jerk," Betsy muttered as Chad spun on his heel and walked away.

"You got that right," Ryan said.

Betsy looked surprised. "You know about him?"

"I know he's got a wife and kids but he's no family man." Ryan met her gaze. "I don't know what he did to you."

Betsy averted her gaze and took a sip of her club soda. Her hand shook slightly. "Who said he did anything?"

"You did." Ryan put a hand on her arm and steered her to a table that a couple had just vacated. It was away from the karaoke stage and far from the three-piece band playing country classics. A quiet spot. Or at least as quiet as it got in Wally's Place.

"I did not."

"You said, and I quote 'You know about him?'"

"That didn't mean anything."

"It did, but you don't have to tell me about it if you don't want to." Though Ryan wanted to know what Chad had done to put the anger in her eyes, he was determined not to press. Until he saw tears form in her eyes.

She blinked rapidly and immediately lowered her gaze to her drink, as if hoping he hadn't noticed.

He'd noticed all right. He placed a hand on her arm. "You can trust me."

She looked up and met his gaze. Something in the liquid blue depths told Ryan he wasn't going to like what she had to say.

"This has to stay here," she said finally. "Just between us."

Ryan nodded. "Understood."

"Chad attacked me in the boardroom."

"He what!?" Ryan shouted. He rose from his seat, but Betsy grabbed his hand and pulled him down.

"Keep your voice down," Betsy ordered. "This is between us, not everyone else in the bar."

"Tell me," Ryan demanded. "Don't leave anything out."

Though he'd been in his share of fights, Ryan wasn't a violent man. But this was his friend's sister and Keenan was, well he wasn't here. Betsy had no one to protect her. No one but him.

"We were working late on a case." Betsy's voice shook slightly.

Ryan tightened his fingers around the edge of the table. *Let her talk*, he told himself, *don't interrupt*.

Betsy glanced down at her club soda and took a deep breath. She lifted her gaze to meet his eyes. "He made remarks about my..." She paused and chewed on her lower lip then glanced down at her chest, "breasts. He has a thing for women who are, ah, generously endowed."

Ryan wasn't quite sure how to respond. Everyone in town knew that in looks she'd taken after her Las Vegas showgirl mother. He hadn't really paid attention to her curvaceous figure

—she was Keenan's sister, for chrissakes—but had no doubt other men had noticed.

"I told him that kind of talk wasn't appropriate. That he was my employer." A bleakness filled her eyes for a second then disappeared. "He laughed and said if it bothered me, I'd have said something long before then."

Ryan chose his words carefully. "Had he made other overtures?"

Betsy gave a jerky nod. "The first day I started, he made some comment about how my dress flattered my figure. It wasn't so much what he said as how he said it. I didn't like the way his gaze lingered on my chest, but I told myself I was simply being overly sensitive."

"Then what happened?" Ryan forced a conversational tone at odds with the anger sluicing through his veins.

"The comments continued, becoming more blatant, more... crude." Betsy's eyes took on a distant look. "I started looking for another job but there was nothing. He was very careful to be perfectly respectful when we were around other people."

"How did you end up alone with him?"

Thankfully she didn't appear to take offense at the question. "One of the other attorneys was with us, but she got a call that her child was sick and had to leave suddenly. We were almost through so I thought it would be okay."

"What happened?" Ryan asked through gritted teeth.

"He started talking about how I wanted it, how I wanted him. I tried to laugh it off but he was, well, he was acting crazy. He lunged at me, tore my silk blouse. I'm not sure how far he would have taken it. I used one of the self-defense moves Keenan had taught me and I got away."

"You should have called the police, charged him with attempted rape."

"It would have been my word against his...and we both know

that his family's reputation in the community is so much better than mine."

"Still—"

She placed a hand on his arm. "He wanted to fire me, but I told him he would give me a good reference and say I was downsized. If he didn't, I'd go to the police."

"The authorities need to know what he did." His lips were stiff and the words sounded as if they were coming from far away.

"Ryan." Her tone took on an urgency. "Listen to me. You don't know what it's like coming from a family like mine. I want to put all that behind me. I don't want to go to court and feel like a victim and then have people look at me and whisper and wonder what I did to encourage him."

Ryan clenched his hands into fists. "I hate the thought of him getting away with this."

"As do I," she said in a sad little voice. "I guess that's how it has to be."

"I suppose…" Ryan fought to keep a lid on the anger rising inside him. The thought of Chad talking to Betsy in that manner, of touching her, made him want to go over to his house and punch him in the nose.

"You promised me," she reminded him.

"I won't do anything."

"Or say anything."

"Or say anything," Ryan reluctantly agreed, not liking this arrangement at all and already trying to think of a way around it. Must be the lawyer in him.

"Thank you." Her hand reached over and covered his, giving it a squeeze. Then, as if realizing what she'd done, she pulled it back. "You know I vowed to never tell anyone about the incident."

"Why?"

"I felt stupid, almost as if I was the guilty one."

"That's how predators like Chad want you to feel."

"I know," she said with a sigh.

"You didn't tell anyone?" A thought struck him. "Not even Adrianna?"

Betsy shook her head.

"Yet you told me."

"Maybe because you were available." She gave a little laugh. "Maybe it was time to get it off my chest."

He winced at the pun and she chuckled.

"Seriously, I feel better."

"I'm glad you feel better." If Chad had been standing in front of him now, Ryan would have decked the guy. "Me? I'm mad as hell."

"I shouldn't have said anything."

"I'm glad you did," he said, realizing it was true. He'd known Betsy as long as he'd known Keenan. He'd watched her struggle to grow up in that difficult home life. She had every reason to be proud of her success in breaking free of her mother's world. "That's what friends are for."

Tears filled her eyes. "Do you really mean that?"

"Absolutely." Ryan looked into her soft blue eyes and made a vow. While Keenan was away, he would be Betsy's champion, her protector and her friend.

As long as he was around, no man was going to even look at her wrong. If they did, they'd answer to him.

CHAPTER FOUR

"That pond-sucking scum." Adrianna's green eyes flashed and she placed the dress back on the rack with extra force.

Betsy had just finished telling her friend the same story she'd told Ryan last night. The way she figured, she couldn't tell him about Chad and keep her best friend in the dark.

When Adrianna had called Saturday morning and mentioned doing some shopping, Betsy had been seriously tempted to beg off. After recounting the tale of that night in the boardroom with Chad, she'd had difficulty sleeping.

She decided nothing would be accomplished by moping in her apartment. But she wasn't in the mood to go over to Aunt Agatha's home--with no heat--and clean.

"Let's not talk about Chad anymore," Betsy said. "He's so not worth the time."

Adrianna met her gaze. "You should file charges."

"That's what Ryan said," Betsy said with a sigh.

"You told Ryan Harcourt the story." Adrianna's eyes widened with disbelief. "Before you told *me*?"

Betsy briefly explained about running into Chad at Wally's Place. "I have to admit I felt better getting it off my chest."

"Why didn't you tell me when it happened?" Hurt underscored Adrianna's words. "You had to know I'd be there for you."

"I was embarrassed," Betsy began then paused when the clerk, who'd been hovering just out of earshot, moved closer.

"Is there anything I can help you ladies find?" the woman asked.

Adrianna flashed her trademark smile at the plump grandmotherly type. "Thank you but we're just looking."

After making them promise to let her know if they needed anything, the woman bustled off to help a customer at the cash register.

"Let's talk about something more pleasant," Betsy said. "Delivered any babies lately?"

It was a question guaranteed to change the subject. Her friend loved her job as a nurse midwife and could talk about it anytime, anywhere.

Adrianna laughed. "All I'm saying is that nine months ago must have been an extremely busy time. It's been crazy lately."

"Maybe one of these days it'll be you or me having a little one." The second the words left her lips Betsy wished she could pull them back. With Adrianna being so commitment-phobic and her being so, well, it wasn't like men were beating down her door, the odds that either one of them would end up with a home and family of their own were decreasing every day.

"Perhaps." Adrianna gave a little shrug, her eyes giving nothing away. "By the way, did I mention that I got a text from Tripp Randall the other day?"

Betsy thought for a moment. "Tall, sandy-haired guy? His dad had cattle?"

"That's the one."

"Does he still live in Jackson Hole?" She hadn't heard the name since she moved back.

"His parents do, but he's been living in Connecticut since he got out of college."

Betsy wasn't surprised. A lot of the people who grew up in Jackson Hole and left for college didn't come back. One thing did surprise her. "Why did he text you?"

"His wife Gayle Doyle and I were friends." Adrianna put down the gold sweater she'd picked up only moments before. Her hands fluttered to her hair, nervously pushing a long strand of chestnut hair back from her face. "We played on the volleyball team together. She was a wing spiker. You could always count on Gayle to make the big play."

If it were anyone else, Betsy would have labeled the talk nervous chatter. But Adrianna *never* chattered.

"You remember Gayle, Bets." Adrianna's eyes were a little too bright.

Betsy thought harder and an image of a vivacious brunette came into focus. Betsy never realized she and Anna were friends.

Acquaintances, yes. But friends? Betsy couldn't remember a single activity Gayle had attended with her and Adrianna.

"So Gayle and Tripp married and now he's texting you." Betsy picked up a tan cardigan. Adrianna shook her head ever-so-slightly and Betsy dropped the sweater back on the stack. "My question is, what does Gayle think of him contacting you?"

Sudden sadness filled Adrianna's eyes. "Gayle died during childbirth four years ago."

Betsy gasped. "I didn't think that kind of thing happened anymore."

"It doesn't. Not often anyway." Adrianna expelled a heavy sigh. "It's always so sad when it does."

"What went wrong?"

"The placenta separated from the uterine wall. There was massive bleeding. Both her and the baby died."

Betsy thought of Gayle with her laughing dark eyes and big smile. She'd always seemed so full of life. Now she was dead. "Did they have other children?"

Adrianna shook her head. "This baby was their first."

"You still didn't say why he contacted you."

"I think he's lonely. He texts me every now and again."

Okay, so the guy was lonely. Betsy noticed her friend hadn't really answered her question. "Sounds to me like he might be on the hunt for a new wife."

Adrianna took extra time inspecting what looked to be a snag in a pair of silk pants. She spoke without lifting her gaze. "Tripp lived down the road from me growing up. He was like a big brother. Sort of like you and Ryan. Same kind of relationship."

Betsy inhaled sharply. She'd often thought that Adrianna suspected she liked Ryan a whole lot more than she let on. Now she was unsure whether the comment meant that Adrianna liked Tripp, as in *really* liked him, or if they were simply friends. She put a hand to her head. This was getting so confusing.

Adrianna placed the pants back on the rack. "Tripp wanted to tell me he was—"

A loud shrill pulsating sound filled the air, drowning out the rest of Adrianna's words.

"I'm sorry, ladies." The clerk reappeared, but this time her friendly smile appeared forced and there were lines of strain around her eyes. "I'm afraid I'm going to have to ask you to vacate the building."

"Is there a fire?" Betsy sniffed the air. She didn't smell smoke or see any flames.

"A fire hasn't been identified." The woman herded them in the direction of the front door as she spoke. "We've had some electrical problems the past few days. I'm sure this is part of that issue. Still, we can't take any chances."

"Of course not," Adrianna murmured.

Once they were out on the sidewalk, Betsy turned toward her friend, eager to hear more. "Tell me—"

Adrianna raised a hand and slipped her cell phone out of her pocket. With the sirens of fire trucks filling the air, Betsy hadn't even heard it ring.

Her friend listened for several seconds, asked a few questions then told the person she was speaking with that she'd be right there.

"What's up?" Betsy asked.

"Baby on the way." Adrianna reached into her bag for her car keys. "Sorry to cut our shopping trip short."

Betsy glanced at the firemen hustling into the boutique. It didn't look like she and Adrianna would have been returning to that store anytime soon. "No worries."

"I'll call you later and we'll set up another time," Adrianna said.

"Then you can tell me all about Tripp," Betsy said pointedly.

"Nothing to tell," Adrianna said over her shoulder as she started down the sidewalk. "Old friend. No big deal."

Betsy opened her bag and took out her keys, pondering the words. *Old friends*. She thought about Ryan. Thought about Adrianna's blasé attitude. Thankfully Tripp lived far away. If he lived close, Betsy might have to warn Adrianna that a girl needed to watch out for old friends. They could be dangerous, very dangerous, to a woman's heart.

The next couple of weeks passed quickly. Betsy and Adrianna talked on the phone but never did find another time to get together. At work, Betsy settled into a comfortable relationship with Ryan.

He treated her like a good friend.

She fell more deeply in love.

Though she tried to hide her feelings, she wondered if he was starting to see through her. Several times in the past few days she'd caught him eying her curiously when he didn't think she was looking.

Today she'd made a concerted effort to keep her distance.

"In the mood for a cappuccino?" he asked unexpectedly as the end of the day loomed.

Betsy would die for a shot of espresso but it wouldn't be wise to encourage such closeness. *Just say no*, she told herself.

"Absolutely," she said. "Do you want me to finish up these documents first?"

"They'll still be here tomorrow." He grabbed her parka from the closet and handed it to her. "You'll need this. The temperature has dropped at least twenty degrees since this morning."

"I haven't been outside," Betsy admitted then swallowed a groan. Ryan had made it clear when she started working for him that she needed to take a lunch break.

He didn't appear to make the connection. His eyes took on a distant, faraway look.

"I met Cole for lunch," Ryan murmured, his mind drifting back to their conversation. Talking with his friend about old football plays had gotten Ryan thinking that an offense-driven approach would be more productive than waiting around.

It was then that he'd begun to formulate his game plan. He wasn't sure how Betsy would react to his declaration but he certainly wasn't making any progress with his current strategy. He could have said something to her in the office, but because it was a personal issue, he wanted to do it in a non-work setting.

Since it was the Tuesday before Thanksgiving and mid-afternoon, Hill of Beans should be fairly deserted. After helping Betsy on with her coat—obviously made to withstand a subarctic blast —he shrugged on his own jacket then opened the door and waited for her to pass.

As she slipped out the door, he caught a whiff of vanilla and smiled. After almost two weeks he'd finally made the connection. Betsy smelled like his mother's kitchen on baking day.

A pleasant scent for a pleasant co-worker. Having Betsy in the office had worked out better than he ever imagined. She was prompt, efficient and managed to somehow anticipate his every need. They were like a well-oiled machine. He hoped today's conversation wouldn't affect that happy balance.

The wind was brisk but thankfully the coffee shop sat just around the corner. Before long they were inside the warm shop with cups of frothy cappuccino before them.

"Got big plans for the Thanksgiving weekend?" he asked.

"Adrianna is having a few people over on Thursday." Betsy took a sip of her drink. "I'm helping."

"I bet you're an excellent cook."

Red crept up her neck, although his comment seemed to please her. "I could be awful."

"You're too competent at everything you do to be awful."

She frowned slightly and took a sip of her drink.

Though he'd meant it as a compliment, for some reason that's not how she'd appeared to have taken it. Since when wasn't "competent" a good thing?

"You're right," she said, finally. "I'm very good in the kitchen. My pumpkin strudel pie is to die for."

"I'd like to try it sometime."

Betsy merely smiled and took another sip of her cappuccino. "What are you doing for the holiday?"

"My plans are up in the air." He'd deliberately turned down Cole and Meg's invitation as well as a Thanksgiving invite from Travis and Mary Karen Fisher. All because he wanted to be available should this conversation go the way he'd hoped. "Betsy, there's something I need to speak with you about."

Her dusty blue eyes met his. For a second all he could think of was how pretty she looked in her pink fluffy sweater. And how her lips looked like plump ripe strawberries. Ryan shook his head to clear the thoughts.

"You're scaring me." Two lines of worry furrowed her brow. "Is it something with my work? If I'm doing anything wrong, just tell me and I'll correct it."

"It's nothing work-related." He offered her a reassuring smile.

"You're doing an awesome job. I don't know what I'd do without you."

She expelled a breath. "Good."

"This is something personal."

Her fingers stilled on the large cup sitting in front of her. "Really?"

While Betsy hadn't given him permission to stray into the personal realm, she hadn't shut the door either. Ryan decided to plunge through the slight opening he'd been given. "I've never had any trouble getting dates. Or talking to women. But when the woman is special to you and she doesn't know she is, finding the right words can be hard."

Betsy simply stared.

"Do you know what it's like to want someone but not be sure if they want you?"

Her eyes never left his face. She nodded slowly.

"To wonder if they only think of you as a friend or if their feelings run as deep as yours but they're afraid to say anything for fear of looking foolish."

"I—" Betsy cleared her throat before continuing, "I can relate."

"Can you?" Ryan reached forward and took her hands.

"A person shouldn't keep feelings like that under wraps." Her voice shook with emotion. "You should always say what you feel."

"Even if I'm not sure the other person feels the same way?"

"How do you know unless you ask?" Two bright spots of pink dotted her cheeks.

Ryan wondered if she'd guessed his secret. "You're right," he said. "I'm going to just blurt it out."

"Tell me, Ryan," she urged. "Tell me what you're feeling."

He took a deep breath. "I'm wanting to date Adrianna Lee but I'm not sure how she feels about me."

A shutter fell across Betsy's eyes. Even when she blinked the shutters remained firmly closed, hiding her thoughts, her reaction from his view. She released his hands and sat back, which he took to be a very bad sign.

"You and Adrianna?" Betsy stumbled over the name. "I thought that you, that we—"

She clamped her mouth shut.

Ryan tilted his head. "Did you think I was talking about you and me?"

Was that pity in his eyes?

Betsy's heart fluttered like a thousand tiny hummingbirds in her chest. Dear God, this was her worst nightmare come to life. She had to find a way to salvage this situation and save her pride.

"You and me?" She somehow managed a respectable sounding laugh. "Pssh. We're just friends."

By the look in his eyes, Betsy knew she hadn't quite allayed his suspicions. How uncomfortable it would be for them to work in the same office day after day if he thought she was pining over him? She had to make him think there was someone else. The question was who? They knew most of the same people.

"As long as we're sharing confessions, I have my own secret crush. That's why I could so easily relate to what you were saying."

The muscles in his shoulders relaxed and the suspicion that had colored his gaze all but disappeared. "Who is he?"

If she refused to tell him, he'd think she was lying. But she couldn't pick anyone currently living in Jackson Hole. That would be way too uncomfortable. She wouldn't put it past Ryan to spill the beans.

Think, she told herself, *think of a name.*

"Tripp Randall."

"The Tripp Randall who used to live here?"

"He lives back east now." Betsy relaxed against the chair, feeling comfortable enough to take a sip of her now lukewarm drink. "He was married, but—"

"—his wife died."

At first Betsy was surprised. How did he know that Tripp's wife has passed away? Then she reminded herself that this was Jackson Hole. It was hard to keep any kind of secret in this town.

"Even though he's now single, I don't think there's any chance of us getting together," Betsy said. "I mean, he's in Connecticut and I'm here."

"Not for much longer."

"What do you mean? I don't have any plans to move."

"You haven't heard?"

"Heard what?"

"I just got a call from him this morning." Ryan smiled. "Tripp is moving back to Jackson Hole."

CHAPTER FIVE

Betsy dressed for work the next morning, still thinking about her conversation with Ryan in the coffee-shop.

She hadn't known what to say when he revealed his feelings for Adrianna. It made perfect sense. Heck if she was a guy, she'd pick Adrianna too. The woman was smart and beautiful. And she had a kind heart.

His announcement had shaken Betsy to the core. Though she'd never admit this to anyone, there had been a few wonderful seconds where she'd been convinced that he was going to declare his love for her. When he said her friend's name instead, she'd wanted to cry. She hadn't. She'd kept her pride.

What if he now thought she was interested in a man she could barely remember? There were worse things, such as him knowing her true feelings.

No, it hadn't been a good day. But if she hadn't thought quickly, it could have been so much worse.

By the time she arrived at work she had her emotions firmly under control. Only eight hours to get through and then she'd have four days away from Ryan. Four days to lick her wounds.

Four days to figure out how she was going to deal with working for a man she loved who had the hots for her best friend.

Ryan was in court all morning. Adrianna had asked Betsy to meet her for lunch. Though she didn't like lying to her friend, her emotions were too raw and she made up an excuse about having too much work to do.

Actually, it was the truth. She was hoping to be able to get her tasks done so she could leave early and minimize the time spent with Ryan.

The clock had just chimed one when Ryan appeared. Betsy smiled and said hello as he walked through the back door, knowing it would have looked odd to do anything else. Then she immediately returned her attention to the papers on her desk, hoping he'd go straight into his adjoining office and shut the door.

He crossed the room and stood by her desk giving her no choice but to look up. "Is there something you need?"

He shifted from one foot to the other. "About our conversation yesterday—"

"All forgotten." She spoke quickly before he could continue.

Ryan dropped into the chair next to her desk. The spicy scent of his cologne teased her nostrils. "I did a lot of thinking last night."

Every muscle in Betsy's body tensed. She had no idea what he was going to say but she had the feeling she wasn't going to like it.

"I've come up with something that might just solve both of our problems." His voice said he was quite pleased with himself.

"I don't have a problem." Betsy picked up the Promissory Note she was working on for one of Ryan's clients, but the words swam before her eyes.

"You like Tripp. You want to be with him. Now he's moving back to Jackson." He smiled expectantly as if he'd just given her all the information she needed tied up in a neat little bow.

The truth was she didn't have a clue what he was trying to say. She wished he would take his enticing smile and his delicious smelling cologne and leave her alone. "While I might like Tripp, he doesn't know I exist."

"You realize this man you like is a good friend of mine."

The man I like is you, you idiot, she wanted to say. Betsy bit her tongue.

"You and I share a common issue," Ryan continued. "Like Tripp, Adrianna doesn't know I exist."

He seemed to expect her to say something so Betsy obliged. "Adrianna is a good friend of mine."

"Exactly." Ryan slapped his hand on the table as if she'd just answered the million-dollar question.

Except...she didn't know the question. "I don't understand."

The look he shot her seemed to say, you're smarter than this. Of course, that wasn't true. Because if she was the least bit intelligent, she'd have stopped herself from falling in love with him.

"Are you familiar with the principle of 'you scratch my back, I'll scratch yours?'"

Betsy slowly nodded.

"Well, you help get me in front of Adrianna," he said with a little smile, "and I get you in front of Tripp. Then we let nature take its course."

"Get in front of..." Betsy dropped the Promissory Note to the desk. This conversation required her full concentration. "What does that exactly mean?"

"For example, you help me spend time with Adrianna. That way she'll have the opportunity to get to know me better. After all, to know me is to love me."

Despite his playful wink, Betsy couldn't manage to summon a smile. "You mean like I'd take you with me to Adrianna's house for Thanksgiving?"

"What a great idea." Ryan practically jumped out of his chair in his enthusiasm. "That's exactly the type of intervention I'm talking about. I want to make it very clear that this wouldn't be one-sided."

"It wouldn't?"

"Absolutely not. Once Tripp is back and settled in, I'll definitely return the favor."

Betsy felt a knot in the pit of her stomach. The fact was she might need an introduction to the man. Though he'd been a friend of Ryan's, she didn't remember Tripp all that well. Unlike Adrianna, she hadn't thought about him since high school. Even back then he hadn't made a big impression. "I don't know..."

"What's not to know? To get someone to fall in love with you, they have to be around you, spend time with you."

The flicker of hope that one day Ryan might wake up and realize she was the woman of his dreams had been all but snuffed out when he'd announced he was interested in Adrianna. Still, she realized now that a tiny spark remained. Which meant she was either a hopeless romantic or the dumbest woman on the face of the earth. Betsy suspected both were true.

Because now, gazing into those beautiful grey eyes she found herself wondering if maybe, just maybe, they spent more time together Ryan would see that it wasn't Adrianna he wanted, but her.

You're going to get your heart broken, a tiny voice of reason in her head whispered. She ignored it. The way Betsy saw it love wasn't for wusses.

"What would make the most sense would be for the two of us to start hanging out together." Betsy forced a slightly bored tone. "We make it clear to everyone that we're just old friends. That way Adrianna and—"

Panic rose inside Betsy. Who was supposed to be her crush? For a split second his name fled her mind.

"Tripp." Ryan filled in the blank.

"Yes, Tripp." She quickly repeated the name ten times in her head so she wouldn't forget it again. "Since we don't want them to think we're a couple or anything..."

"No, we don't want that." Ryan spoke a little too quickly for her liking.

"Anyway, it would seem less suspicious. I know that Adrianna--" Betsy paused for effect, "wouldn't think it strange at all if you started coming around with me."

Betsy vowed in that moment, if Ryan and Adrianna discovered that they were soul mates, she'd be happy for them. Even while her heart was breaking, she'd never let it show on her face.

Ryan's expression turned thoughtful. As he drummed his fingers on the table, she could almost see him considering the pros and cons of what she'd suggested. "I think it would work," he said finally. "Tripp would be less suspicious, too."

Her gaze met his. "Please know that if we give it our best shot and he doesn't return my feelings, I'm not the type to cling or to be where I'm not wanted."

The words flowed from her heart and they were as much for her sake as for the attorney sitting beside her. It wasn't Tripp who needed to know this about her, it was Ryan.

Betsy jumped when his hand closed over hers. "You're a wonderful woman. He'd be crazy not to want you."

Her skin turned hot beneath his touch. Even as she hugged the words close to her heart, Betsy found herself wondering if he thought she was so wonderful, why didn't Ryan want her for himself? She slipped her hand out from beneath his. "Sounds like we have a deal."

Ryan rubbed his chin. "When should we start?"

"Adrianna is having a few friends over for Thanksgiving dinner tomorrow. I'll tell her to set the table for one more. Unless you're busy—"

"I'll be there," he said immediately. "What time shall I pick you up?"

"Five o'clock would be fine."

"I've got a good feeling about this," Ryan said.

Well, Betsy thought, *that makes one of us.*

~

The next morning, while making a sweet potato casserole, Betsy made her own pro-con list in her head. She still hadn't told Adrianna that Ryan was coming because she wasn't sure she was going through with their agreement. Food wouldn't be a problem if she did decide to go along with his scheme and let him come. There was plenty to eat.

Even after she'd finished with the food preparation, she still wasn't certain the pros outweighed the cons. But later that afternoon, she realized she had no choice. Not unless she wanted Ryan to know it was him she liked, not Tripp.

She called Adrianna and told her she'd like to bring Ryan with her. Just as she thought Adrianna hadn't minded. In fact she'd been rather enthusiastic. Though Betsy had stressed that Ryan was simply a friend, she got the feeling Adrianna didn't believe her. It was at that point Betsy thought about coming clean and telling her friend about the crazy scheme Ryan had concocted.

Several things stopped her. She'd given Ryan her word to keep this arrangement just between them. In this day of easy promises, she liked to think that her word meant something. And then there was a more practical matter. If she went back on her promise, what would stop Ryan from going back on his word? If he told Tripp Randall that she was interested in him, she'd be mortified.

She glanced at the medallion lying on the dresser. This was her chance to get to know Ryan better and for him to get to know her in a non-work environment. Perhaps she'd discover he wasn't her one true love. Then she could move on with her life. Find the man she was meant to be with.

What if she didn't get tired of him? She decided to give this odd arrangement until the holidays were over. If he hadn't fallen for her by then, he never would. Then she would make every effort to do as she'd promised and steer Adrianna his way. Until then, she was giving herself the best shot.

The ringing of her doorbell pulled her from her reverie. She glanced at the clock on the wall surprised to find it was time. Taking one last quick look in the mirror, she was pleased to see that for an average person, she looked a little above average today.

She paired a soft red sweater with a black pencil skirt and heels. Even if she had to say it herself, she looked pretty darn good.

The doorbell rang again and Betsy swiped on another layer of lip gloss. She shut Puffy, her Pomeranian, in the bedroom before hurrying to the door.

Betsy's breath caught in her throat as the door swung open. Above average was today's ugly duckling. Next to Ryan she was a brown moth with nothing to recommend her.

For the casual dinner this evening Ryan was once again dressed all in black. Black sweater. Black pants. Black boots. Few guys could pull such a look off but on him it worked. Broad shoulders, lean hips and classically handsome features. His hair was tousled and still slightly damp from the shower. He looked, well, way out of her league.

"Happy Thanksgiving." He leaned forward and brushed a kiss across her cheek.

Betsy went absolutely still, resisting—but barely—the urge to touch the tingling spot where his lips had just been.

"What, what was that for?"

His eyes widened ever so slightly. "It's a holiday and you looked so nice." Concern filled his eyes. "Was I out of line?"

Mutely, she shook her head.

"Really, if you think I was even the least little bit, just slug me." He leaned over, sticking out his chin.

Betsy raised her hand, but instead of clenching it into a fist, she cupped his face and kissed him right on the lips, like she'd been longing to do for years.

He responded immediately. His lips were warm and firm and he tasted faintly like chewing gum. When she pulled back, a tiny smile tugged at his lips. "What was that for?

Betsy shrugged and reached for her coat. "You looked so nice," she said mimicking his response to her, "and it is, after all, a holiday."

The rest of the tension left his face. He grinned. "And I'm starving."

"You and me both."

He helped her on with her parka. His fingers brushed her neck and a curious thrumming filled her veins. She wasn't sure what had gotten in her but she was happy she'd taken advantage of the opportunity. Because when this was all over, she didn't want to have any regrets. Right now, she didn't have a one.

Somehow Betsy ended up across the table from Ryan at dinner while Adrianna sat directly to his right. He wasn't sure how much Betsy had to do with the seating arrangement but he owed her big time for this.

The beautiful brunette had smiled a welcome when he'd walked through the door with Betsy. She'd thanked him warmly when he'd handed her a bottle of wine. It had to be the fact that he was here as a guest of her best friend that made the difference. Whatever it was, he appreciated Betsy's efforts. Once Tripp was in town and settled, he would definitely return the favor.

Betsy was telling a hilarious story about the time she and her brother had gotten lost at Yellowstone. He wondered if she knew how pretty she looked when she smiled. He had the feeling he wouldn't have to do much pushing to get Tripp to notice her.

Although Ryan liked Tripp, he was surprised Betsy had a thing for him. He just didn't seem her type. Ryan pulled his brows together and stabbed a piece of, ugh, purple asparagus.

"Does the asparagus taste okay?" Adrianna whispered to him. "I made it myself."

Her perfume was sultry, a sexy fragrance he usually loved. Tonight, he found himself wondering if she'd ever considered wearing something different, lighter, say a vanilla scent. For some reason that fragrance held more appeal.

"Everything is...wonderful," he said, looking into her beautiful green eyes. "My favorite is the sweet potato casserole."

"Betsy made it." Adrianna smiled proudly.

"How?" he asked. "We didn't bring any food with us."

We? Us? Using words like that made it seem that he and Betsy were a couple. Hardly the impression he wanted to give to Adrianna. Thankfully she didn't appear to notice.

"Betsy is a fabulous cook." Adrianna's long slender fingers curved around the wine glass as she lifted it to her full lips and took a sip. "She came over this morning and helped me get the dinner together. Left to my own talents, this feast would not have been nearly so delightful."

Ryan's admiration for Adrianna inched up another notch. Not many women would be so generous with their praise. He had the feeling she cooked much better than she was admitting.

"Betsy is a special woman." Adrianna smiled in her friend's direction.

"She's a good friend." Ryan put extra emphasis on the last word, not wanting there to be any misunderstanding.

"It's been hard on her, having Keenan...gone." The corners of Adrianna's lips lifted when Betsy laughed at something Benedict Campbell said. "I like seeing her happy."

Ryan nodded absently; his attention suddenly drawn to Betsy. He didn't like the way that Ben was looking at her. The prominent Jackson Hole orthopedic surgeon was known for being a love 'em and leave 'em kind of guy. He wondered if Betsy was aware of that fact. Perhaps he'd have to find a way to bring it to her attention on the drive home. It was a good thing she was interested in Tripp. He wouldn't want her falling for Benedict.

"When Betsy called, I sensed she was concerned that I might not want you here."

Ryan reluctantly jerked his attention back to Adrianna. It almost looked as if Ben had placed his hand on Betsy's knee. He told himself that wasn't his concern. He was here to make a good impression on Adrianna and to mend that long-ago rift. His hostess had just given him the perfect opportunity to discuss that incident. He needed to take advantage of it and not worry so much about Betsy. Still, he kept one eye focused in her direction.

"I'm sorry about the high school incident," he said to Adrianna. The regret in his voice was real. He hadn't known she'd be in the middle of changing her clothes when he'd led the charge into the locker room. "Truly if I knew you—"

"--didn't have any clothes on—"

"--I never would have entered the locker room." His voice was low, for her ears only. "Please accept my apology."

Her gaze narrowed. She searched his eyes. Then a smile lifted her lips. "Accepted."

Ryan reached over and took her hand, lifting it to his lips. "Thank you."

Satisfaction flowed through him when she didn't pull away. Her skin was warm and smooth beneath his lips. He found he couldn't fully enjoy the moment.

Not with Benedict holding Betsy's hand, right across the table from him, with that familiar predatory gleam in his eyes.

CHAPTER SIX

"She accepted my apology," Ryan handed Betsy a glass of wine and sank into her sofa. He ignored the Pomeranian's growl of displeasure.

After they'd left Adrianna's, Betsy invited him to her apartment for a recap of the evening. Outside, snow had begun to fall in earnest but Ryan scarcely noticed. Betsy's apartment was warm and inviting. Unlike most of the women he knew, her place had a homey, rather than a designer feel.

There were rag rugs on the hardwood floors and the furniture had that comfortable lived-in look and feel. Her coffee table was rugged with various nicks and stains. When he asked if she had a coaster before he sat down his beer can, she'd waved a hand and told him not to worry.

She'd flipped on a couple of table lamps that cast a golden glow to the room, making confidences come more easily. He'd just relayed his conversation with Adrianna. Ryan couldn't wait to hear what she had to say about Benedict. He lifted the can of beer to his lips but didn't take a sip. "So what was going on with you and Benedict?"

"He's a nice guy. We were just talking." She waved a dismissive hand. "Did you like the dinner?"

"It was good. Adrianna said you made most of it."

"I helped," Betsy said modestly. "Cooking is a passion of mine."

"My favorite was the sweet potato casserole."

Betsy paused. Were they really going to sit here and talk about the food? When there were so many more important things to discuss?

She swallowed past the lump in her throat. "I saw you kiss Adrianna's hand."

He took a sip of beer before speaking. "Do you think it was too much?"

Was he really asking her for dating advice? She, who hadn't been out on a date in almost a year? She was willing to help him out but not now. Not this way. Not until she'd given herself a fair chance.

"Trust me. You don't want to rush Adrianna."

"Okay. I'll keep that in mind."

To her surprise Ryan didn't seem all that upset. He was a strange one. Like tonight. Unless it was just her overactive imagination, she could have sworn that he'd spent more of the evening watching her than flirting with Adrianna.

"Do you want to play Monopoly?"

Betsy jerked her thoughts back to the present. "What?"

"Monopoly. I haven't played in years. I see it on your shelf."

Betsy followed his gaze. There was a bookcase against the wall filled with games and puzzles. She didn't know what surprised her most. That Ryan had wanted to come in her apartment in the first place. Or that he appeared to be in no hurry to leave.

She wasn't complaining. Hadn't she just this morning made a vow to get to know him better? And let him get to know her?

"Sure," she said, rising to her feet. "But I've got to tell you one thing first."

"What is that?"

Her lips curved up in broad smile. "I play to win."

Two hours later, Ryan landed on Park Place. He let out a groan that could be heard around the world. The rent for the hotel Betsy had placed on the expensive property took the rest of his money. He leaned back against the soft fabric sofa. "You're one tough businesswoman, Ms. McGregor."

Betsy scooped up the paper bills. "It's a pleasure taking your cash, Mr. Harcourt."

"Shyster," he said beneath his breath.

"What did you say?"

"I said I'd be happy to help you pick up."

"Yeah, it sounded like that."

They worked together to put all the pieces of the game back together. Ryan couldn't believe how relaxed he had been all evening. Even though they'd eaten a big dinner, Betsy had brought out some homemade Snickerdoodle cookies and they'd munched on those while playing the game. She hadn't even objected when he'd asked if they could have the football game on in the background.

To his surprise she was as much of a football fanatic as he was. Yes, he decided. It had been a good evening. Now he was going to have to brave the cold and the icy streets and head home alone.

At least he'd only had two beers and those were hours ago. After finishing the one Betsy had given him when he arrived, he'd switched to milk, which went better with cookies anyway.

Betsy scrambled to her feet and put the game away.

He stood, oddly reluctant to have the evening end. "I can't remember a nicer Thanksgiving. Thanks for inviting me."

She retrieved his coat from the hall closet. "I had a good time, too."

He wanted to ask her what she was doing this weekend, but thought better of it. Besides it shouldn't really be her plans he should be inquiring about; it should be Adrianna's. "Is it okay if I give you a call tomorrow?"

Betsy nodded. "I'll be around."

Ryan shrugged on his coat, making sure the zipper was all the way up. When he walked out of Betsy's front door, he'd be outside. No enclosed hallway or common foyer for this apartment complex. No covered parking. While Ryan hadn't looked outside lately, he had no doubt the weather had worsened.

He reached for the knob but stopped when he felt her hand on his sleeve.

"Drive safe," she said, her eyes dark and unreadable. "The roads are bound to be snow packed by now."

Ryan turned the knob and reluctantly pulled the door toward him then pushed open the storm. The wind immediately tore the door from his hands, flinging it against the siding. Snow filled the air, whipping against his face, making it difficult to see. With Herculean effort he finally got both doors shut, then paused to wipe the ice particles from his face. "I thought the forecasters said we were only getting a dusting. It's a blizzard out there."

Betsy's brows pulled together in a worried frown. "You can't drive home in that."

"I don't see that I have another option." He pulled the gloves from his pocket, praying he'd put the scraper back in his truck's cab.

"You're not going anywhere." Betsy lifted her chin. "I won't allow it."

"Why, Miss Betsy," Ryan said in an exaggerated Southern drawl. "Are you inviting me to spend the night?"

"I'm not inviting," she said, in a matter-of-fact tone, "I'm telling. You're staying here with me where you'll be safe."

An image flashed through his head. Him and Betsy, cuddled under the mounds of quilts he'd seen on her bed when he'd used the bathroom earlier.

They wouldn't have any clothes on, of course. Everyone knew that you generated more body heat skin-to-skin.

Sleeping with Betsy would make no sense on so many counts that it would be difficult to name them all. If he was going to get naked with anyone, it would be Adrianna. "I'm not sleeping in your bed."

"I don't recall offering that option." Betsy jerked her head in the direction of the sofa. "It's a sleeper, so you should be comfortable. I know this place isn't as big or as nice—"

He put two fingers over her lips silencing her words. "I like it here. I feel comfortable. Especially once the little red fluffball quit growling at me."

"Puffy is going through a difficult time. Aunt Agatha was her whole world. She simply needs a little TLC and time to adjust."

From several things Betsy had said during the game, Ryan knew she hadn't planned on having a dog. Not only because of the expense but because she wasn't home all that often. Despite those issues she'd taken the ten-year-old dog into her home and into her heart because it was the right thing to do.

According to Betsy, her Great-Aunt had loved Puffy as if the dog were her own child. There was no way Betsy was letting her go to the pound or to a stranger. Ryan doubted any of the women he'd dated would make such a sacrifice.

Even Adrianna.

It didn't take long until they were both ready for bed. Betsy gave him a pair of pajamas she'd bought in case Keenan was ever able to visit. When she pushed them into his hands, Ryan accepted, thankful he and his friend were the same size.

She went into her bedroom to change. When she came out, he did a double take. Flannel feet pajamas? "I haven't seen a pair of those since I was four years old."

Her cheeks turned bright pink. "They keep my feet warm."

"You're not going to impress anyone wearing that get-up to bed."

She lifted her chin in a defiant tilt. "You're the only one I see here now and I'm certainly not trying to impress you."

Despite her bravado, he could see that he'd hurt her feelings, which wasn't his intent at all. The truth was, seeing her in such a get-up made his fingers itch to take it off of her, to see the creamy flesh beneath, to touch her, to kiss her all over...

He pulled his thoughts up short. Seeing Adrianna and having such a pleasant conversation with her this evening must have sent his hormones surging.

"I was just thinking of you and Tripp," Ryan said. "Most guys like silky, sheer stuff."

"I appreciate your advice." Her tone said she didn't appreciate it at all. "I think I can be trusted to handle my own love life. Good night, Ryan."

Crossing the room, she kissed him on the lips, like she'd done earlier. Only this time she let her lips linger for an extra heartbeat. "Sleep tight."

"You, too," he called out as she flicked off the lights and headed to her room.

He crawled under the covers and pulled them up to his chin. Betsy might look like a sweet innocent miss but she sure knew how to kiss.

Tripp Randall, he thought to himself, better prepare to be dazzled.

～

Even though they'd been up late the night before, Puffy was ready to go outside at seven am. Betsy tiptoed into the living room, holding the dog in her arms, hoping she wouldn't wake Ryan.

She cast a glance at the couch when she slipped past it. His hair was all mussed and stubble graced his lean cheeks. His eyes were shut and he was breathing easily. From the position of the covers, it looked like he hadn't moved a muscle all night.

He was still sleeping by the time Betsy brought Puffy inside. She took the dog into the bedroom with her where Puffy burrowed under the covers and quickly fell back asleep. Betsy wasn't so lucky.

All she could think of was Ryan lying in the other room. When they'd begun the evening, she hadn't been sure she'd get to see him today. Now here he was. In her apartment. Sleeping. With her.

Well, technically, not with her. He'd just happened to get stranded at her place. They'd had a good time last night. And she'd learned a lot.

As they played the game, they'd started talking about the people they'd dated in the past. She hadn't realized before then just how many women Ryan had dated.

What if he did fall in love with her? Would she always worry that he'd fall out of love as quickly as he fell into it?

"We're not even close to being at that point," Betsy said to Puffy. "There's no need worrying about it...right?"

The Pomeranian stared at her for a long moment then licked her chin.

Tears sprang to Betsy's eyes. She couldn't help it. Sometimes she felt so alone. How long had it been since she'd had someone in her life? Someone she truly cared about?

Keenan. He was in prison.

Aunt Agatha. She was dead.

Ryan. Who considered her simply a means to an end.

But she was going to change that, right? There was no way he could fall for her if he spent the rest of the morning in bed.

"Time to get up," she called out. "We're going to—"

The words died in her throat when she saw Ryan, all tall dark and handsome, standing in the doorway to her bedroom, still in Keenan's pajamas.

"What are we going to do?" He stifled a yawn.

Betsy's heart fluttered in her chest. "I thought I'd make breakfast. Later, maybe we could build a snowman."

It had been an impulsive thought and the second the words left Betsy's mouth she wished she could pull them back. Though her parka and mittens would keep her toasty warm no matter what the temperature, her cheeks would get chapped and her nose would turn a red that would rival Rudolph's. Hardly a way to make an impression. She should take a clue from Adrianna. Her friend wouldn't be caught dead playing in the snow.

"Snowman?"

"Of course if you can't stay or aren't interested I completely understand," she said quickly.

"No, I'm interested."

Her heart nearly stopped when he crossed the room and sat on the bed. He rubbed his arms up and down with his hands. "Jeesh, it's cold in here."

"I keep the temperature at fifty-eight," Betsy admitted. "Saves on heating costs."

"I bet it does."

Before she knew what was happening, he'd flung aside the covers and slipped into bed beside her. Puffy growled but moved over to make room for him.

"What-what are you doing?" Betsy stammered.

"What does it look like?" Ryan said. "I'm preventing myself from getting frostbite while we discuss our plans for the day."

"Oh." Betsy forced herself to breathe. While a tad awkward, this was no different than sitting across the table from him talking over a cup of coffee. Right? *Wrong.* The desire to fling her leg over his and plant an open-mouthed kiss on his neck told Betsy that much.

"What shall we have for breakfast?" he asked in a husky voice that did strange things to her insides. "Cereal?"

Betsy made a face. "I was thinking more along the lines of eggs, bacon and brioche French toast."

"Sounds good to me," Ryan said. "Then what?"

"Nothing." Betty stammered, finding it difficult to think with him so close.

"You said something about building a snowman," he prompted, proving despite that sleepy look he'd been listening.

"I haven't done it in years," she admitted. "It's not much fun building them alone."

Sheesh, Bets. Why not just paint a big "L" on your forehead.

"I think we should build one." He gave a decisive nod. "You know what else?"

Betsy shook her head, unable to keep from staring at those luscious lips of his.

"We should call and ask Adrianna to join us."

CHAPTER SEVEN

Betsy felt as if she'd been punched in the stomach. She hadn't seen that one coming. Still, she didn't think Ryan noticed her surprise. Because of her mother's shocking behavior, she'd had years of practice schooling her features.

"What a good idea," she said brightly. "I'll give Adrianna a call right now."

Pushing the sheets and comforter aside, Betsy hopped out of bed, not even minding the coolness of the air. All she knew was she had to put some distance between her and Ryan. Give herself a few seconds to compose her thoughts and her emotions.

This is what you agreed to, she told herself as she scurried from the room to get her phone. You're supposed to be fixing him up with her. Last night they were two buddies hanging out. When he'd slid into bed with her this morning, her hopes had risen, but he'd only wanted to stay warm. He hadn't given her a second thought. How could he when his thoughts were so firmly focused on Adrianna?

Betsy located her phone in its usual spot, next to the coffee pot on the counter. She took several deep breaths while she unplugged it from the charger then speed dialed Adrianna.

Her friend answered on the first ring. They chatted for a few seconds before the conversation ended.

"Did you reach Adrianna?" Ryan asked from the kitchen doorway, Puffy standing beside him.

"She can't come." Betsy tried not to let her relief show. She wasn't surprised. Adrianna hated driving on snow-packed roads. If a baby was on the way, she went out. Otherwise, she stayed at home. "She has the day off and wants to relax and enjoy it, not play in the white stuff."

A startled look crossed Ryan's face. "She said that?"

"Those were her exact words." Betsy grabbed a sack of coffee from the cupboard and held it up. "Care for a jump start? I have to warn you, I drink the extra-strong Cowboy Blend."

Ryan grinned. "A woman after my own heart. Bring it on, baby."

For someone supposedly so into Adrianna, the attorney didn't seem all that upset that she wasn't joining them. He whistled as he crossed the room with Puffy trotting alongside him. When he reached the table, he paused. "Should I get dressed first?"

"What do you mean?" Betsy dumped some dry dog foot into a bowl with tiny bones around the perimeter then placed it on the floor.

"My mother." Ryan's lips lifted in a rueful smile. "She was very strict with us boys. No food until we were fully dressed."

Betsy thought of her own mom. It had been the same in her house, except she and Keenan didn't get food unless they made it themselves. "Well, I'm not your mother—"

"Thank God—"

"—and I've been known to spend the whole day in my pj's.

His eyes lit up. "Watching football?"

"When the Broncos are playing." Betsy started the coffee and almost instantly a rich aroma filled the air. "Usually I read."

"Do you have any big plans for today?"

"Not until later." She held up a mug. "Black or with cream or sugar?"

"Black, please."

She filled the cup then placed it before him. "With all the sales, I probably should be shopping but it's not like I have anyone to buy for. Except Adrianna and I already know what I'm getting her."

"What about me?" He took a sip of the steaming brew.

Betsy added a dollop of cream to her coffee then took a seat at the table across from him. "Are you asking if you should get Adrianna a gift?"

"Actually, I was asking if you were going to get *me* a gift."

"Dream on, bossman. You make a heckava lot more money than I do."

Ryan grinned and wrapped his hands around the mug. "Can't blame a guy for wanting something under the tree."

Betsy laughed. Ryan had parents, brothers and a boatload of friends. She seriously doubted the guy had to worry about not getting any presents. "Well, if you end up with no gifts, I'll bring one to put under your tree."

"First I have to have one."

"You've lost me."

"A tree." He straightened in his chair so quickly coffee spilled over the top of his cup. "That's what we should do today. Pick out a Christmas tree. One for your place and one for mine."

She handed him a napkin. "I don't put up a tree."

"Why not?" He looked up from the spill, his eyes wide, as if she'd said something horrifying like she didn't eat meat or didn't know how to ski.

The truth was Betsy didn't feel like telling him the holidays had never been a particularly happy time for her. The last time they'd had a tree, she'd been seven. Her mother had come home drunk and fallen into it. "Who'd see it?"

Ryan sat back in his chair, an expression of faux shock on his face. "A scrooge. That's what you are, Betsy McGregor. A modern-day scroogette."

Though he was clearly teasing, something in his tone must have hit Puffy wrong. The Pomeranian lifted her head from the food bowl and growled.

"It's okay, Puffball," Ryan said. "Just keeping it real."

After a moment the dog resumed eating.

"You call me a scrooge simply because I don't put up a Christmas tree?" Betsy laughed. "That's reaching, Harcourt."

"There was a distinct scrooge-like quality to your voice," Ryan insisted, all serious. It was the twinkle in his eyes that gave him away.

"Hey, I'm a romantic. A woman who loves doggies and kitties and small children. I even carry around a coin with hearts on it in my purse."

Ryan leaned back in his chair, a smirk on his face. "You're bluffing."

"Oh, ye of little faith." She grabbed her bag from beside the counter and reached inside. Her fingers quickly located the medallion in the small inner pocket where she'd put it for safe keeping. She pulled it out and tossed it to him.

He caught it easily, flipping it over then holding it up to the light. "This is a Love Token."

"You're making that up."

"I'm not. My father found one in an antique store and bought it for my mother for Valentine's Day a couple years back."

"What's a Love Token?"

"They were popular in the 18th and 19th centuries. It was a coin a man personalized for the woman he loved."

"This one has writing on it, too," Betsy pointed out.

"It's French," he said. "If those years of college French were worth anything, I should be able to translate."

Betsy got up and rounded the table, peering over his shoulder. "What does it say?"

"Vous et Nul Autre," he murmured. "You and No Other."

"What?"

"That's what it says, 'you and no other.'" His eyes softened. "Whoever had this engraved was obviously very much in love."

Betsy loved the sentiment. "You think it's stupid."

To her surprise the smile left his lips. He shook his head, suddenly serious. "Not at all. I hope to feel that way about the woman I marry. I hope she'll feel that same way about me."

Though he didn't say her name, from the look in his eyes Betsy knew Ryan was thinking about Adrianna.

That feeling of closeness that had begun to build, disappeared. "Ready for breakfast?"

"You still need a tree."

"So you say."

Ryan met her gaze. "I'm not giving up."

Betsy steeled her resolve. "I'm not either."

As she got out the skillet, Betsy knew she wasn't talking about a tree. Rather she was talking about the man sitting across the table, the one she loved.

You and no other.

Give up? Not on her life. Not as long as there was a chance he could love her, too.

Ryan had known a lot of women over the last fifteen years. None of them like Betsy. Most of them barely knew what a kitchen was, much less their way around it. Adrianna had been right. Betsy was a fabulous cook. The breakfast she'd made had been the best he'd ever tasted.

Each egg had been a perfect sunny-side up, the bacon crisp without being brittle and the brioche French toast, well even though he was full, his mouth watered just thinking of it now. Her talents didn't end in the kitchen.

She had a keen eye. After she'd showered and he'd cleaned up the kitchen, they'd driven to a Christmas Tree Farm not far from Jackson. With it being Black Friday, there weren't many searching for a tree.

Ryan found one almost immediately, but Betsy had shaken her head and pronounced it too tall. Then he'd found a tree that was beautifully shaped; wide and full. She'd dismissed it as too short.

For someone who hadn't even wanted a tree, she was being awfully picky.

"I've found it," he heard her call out.

He quickened his steps which wasn't easy because of the snow on the ground. Yet it was beautiful outside. The day was clear and the breeze, while cool, had that crisp bite he'd always liked. Overhead the sun shone brightly in a blue sky.

Ryan followed the sound of her voice, grabbing onto a tree branch to help him make his way up a steep slope, wondering how she'd made it. Ryan could see by her tracks that she'd slipped and inched her way up the incline while he was checking out trees further down. She hadn't complained or called to him for help.

He finally made it close enough to get a good view of the tree that had met with her approval. It was a Douglas Fir, thick without being stubby, tall but not straggly. A perfect specimen. Sort of like the woman who stood beside it with her head cocked.

"This one has it all," she said with a decisive nod.

"It will do."

Betsy nodded again. "Now we have to find one for you."

Ryan frowned. "I thought this would be mine."

Betsy's lips twitched. "Nope."

She looked a bit too self-satisfied for his liking.

"Since it's yours..." Ryan grabbed a handful of snow, packed it slightly then let it fly.

It sailed past Betsy's head and splatted against the tree.

Betsy whirled. "Hey, what do you think you're doing?"

"Testing how your perfect tree handles snow load."

"Well, stop it."

"Not yet." Without pausing, Ryan quickly made another snowball. This one clipped the top of the tree.

He smiled. How long had it been since he'd made a snowball, much less thrown one? He really should get—

Snow hit his chest.

Giggles filled the air.

He fixed his gaze on Betsy. "Did you deliberately hit me with that snowball?"

She shook her head, while doubling over with laughter.

"You know what that means…." He scooped another handful of snow and carefully packed it, his gaze never leaving hers.

Her laughter ceased. She straightened and her eyes flashed a warning. "You wouldn't dare."

His smile widened. "You started it."

He released his snowball the instant she released hers. He aimed for her chest. Hers hit him right in the face.

From that second it was game on. The balls flew fast and furious. Ryan bobbed and weaved, but Betsy had a deadly aim. After several minutes, even with gloves, his hands felt frozen and his cheeks stung from where she'd nailed him. Three times. But he was having so much fun he didn't want it to end.

"Stop this right now." The portly owner of the Christmas Tree Farm huffed and puffed his way up the hill, giving a little yelp as Betsy's last snowball barely missed him. "What the heck is going on here?"

"She's got a wicked arm," Ryan said, only half joking. Because he had the snowball in his hand, it seemed a shame to waste it. He let it fly.

"That was unfair, Harcourt," Betsy called out. "He'd said to stop."

"Good to know you're a woman who follows the rules." He knew he shouldn't push his luck, but he couldn't help it.

"I'm going to—" She reached over to grab some snow, but the owner held up his hand.

"If I see one more snowball flying through the air, I'm not letting either of you have a tree."

Ryan thought of how long it had taken them to find even one acceptable specimen. "Truce."

"I'm the winner," Betsy announced.

"You two can discuss that later," the owner said. "Did you find a tree you wanted? Or were you too busy hitting each other with snowballs?"

Betsy caught Ryan's eye and they burst out laughing.

The old man looked at them like they'd lost their mind.

Twenty minutes later, the tree had been cut and placed in the back of Ryan's pick-up. When he saw Betsy shivering, Ryan nixed looking for a second tree.

"One's enough," he told her. "For today. Besides I'd like to get out of these wet clothes. I imagine you would, too."

"I am a bit chilled." Betsy hunched her shoulders against the wind.

"I'll drop you and the tree off at your place, then I'll go home, shower and come back. We can hang the ornaments tonight."

"Uh, actually, Adrianna and I are getting together this evening." Betsy glanced at the blue sky. "Since the weather is better, I'm sure she'll be coming over."

Ryan thought about suggesting that the three of them put up the tree. He decided not to force the issue. "Do you two have big plans for the evening?"

Betsy lifted one shoulder in a slight shrug. "I'm not sure."

"Since it's Friday night, I'll be at Wally's Place. At least for a little while." Ryan kept his tone casual and off-hand. "If you're out you should stop by."

Betsy made a non-committal noise and changed the subject.

They chatted easily on the way to her house. He hadn't realized she was such a rodeo fan.

"Do you miss it?" Betsy asked.

"I miss the adrenalin rush," he admitted. "There's nothing like being on the back of a two-thousand-pound bull and making it a full eight seconds."

"Why did you quit?" From the look in her eye, she was truly interested.

"It's hard on your body," he conceded. "I was fortunate that I'd never been seriously injured. But it was only a matter of time. Besides, I was ready to move on to something else, to the next phase of my life."

"You're a good attorney," Betsy said. "You care about your clients and about seeing justice served."

"My professional life is solid."

"So what's next?"

"Hopefully marriage and a family," Ryan said.

"That's what I want, too."

"That's why we're working together," he reminded her. "To help each other get that special person."

"Adrianna."

"Don't forget Tripp," Ryan said. "On that front, I have some good news."

She glanced out the window.

"I got a text from him while we were looking for a tree. He should be back in Jackson Hole any day. Good news, huh?"

"I guess."

Was that a sigh? "You don't sound very excited."

"I'm realistic," Betsy said. "He won't like me."

Up ahead the light changed to red and Ryan pulled the truck to a stop. "What are you saying? He's going to love you. You're the kind of woman any man would want."

"I'm not that kind of woman," Betsy said, almost sounding

angry. "I'm a buddy. A friend. Someone they can tell their troubles to and then go back to their girlfriend feeling better."

Ryan thought how enticing she'd looked on that hill with her cheeks red with the cold, her eyes as blue as the sky. He wasn't even her boyfriend and it had been all he could do to keep from kissing her.

"Trust me," he said. "Tripp is going to take one look at you... and it'll be all over."

And if Tripp couldn't see what a gem Betsy was, well, he didn't deserve her.

CHAPTER EIGHT

After ordering at the Perfect Pizza front counter, Betsy and Adrianna found a small table by the window and sat down with their drinks.

"I'm glad it quit snowing." Adrianna barely glanced at the outdoor winter wonderland that resembled the front of a Christmas card. Snow clung to bare tree branches while strings of brightly-colored lights decorated the nearby storefronts. "I don't like driving when the roads are slick, but I hated the thought of missing our 'girls' night out.'"

"What did you do all day?" Betsy asked.

"Slept late, did my nails, read a couple issues of Maternal-Fetal Medicine that I hadn't gotten to yet."

"Wild day."

Adrianna's cherry red lips tilted upward. "I'm betting yours wasn't much more exciting."

"Actually, it was," Betsy took a sip of her soda then filled Adrianna in on everything that had happened since they'd last spoken.

Her friend's green eyes widened. "You let him spend the night?"

"He didn't sleep in my bed, if that's what you're intimating." Betsy had conveniently left out the part when he'd crawled under the covers with her that morning. "What was I to do? Throw him out into a blizzard when I have a perfectly nice sofa-bed?"

"I suppose not," Adrianna grudgingly admitted.

"We played monopoly."

"I know that smile. You won, didn't you?" Her friend leaned forward, resting her elbows on the table. "You bought a bunch of properties and put hotels on all of them. He landed on them one too many times and went bankrupt."

Betsy lifted one shoulder and batted her eyelashes. "Perhaps."

Adrianna chuckled. "I'm surprised he's still speaking to you."

"He took it like a gentleman." Betsy realized with a start that Ryan hadn't been at all threatened by her success. "I think he admired my business acumen."

"You need to hold onto him, Bets," her friend said, suddenly serious. "You should consider making him your boyfriend instead of simply your friend."

Oh, if it were only that easy. "He's not interested in me in that way."

"He wouldn't be spending so much time with you if that were true. I've seen how he looks at you."

"Well, I've seen how he looks at *you*," Betsy blurted out.

"Small, thin crust, green and black olive." The college student who'd appeared out of nowhere to stand at the edge of the table, held out the pizza.

"That's ours." Betsy welcomed the interruption. Hopefully by the time they started eating Adrianna would forget all about their Ryan conversation.

The speculative gleam in her friend's eyes to her that was simply wishful thinking.

Adrianna delicately forked off a bite of the pizza. "Are you saying you think Ryan likes *me*?"

"You're his type, Anna. You've got the look he goes for. Perfect hair. Immaculate make-up. Stylish clothes." She couldn't say more without betraying Ryan's confidence.

"That's really gone well for him, hasn't it?"

"What do you mean?"

"He's dated a lot of women since he's been back in Jackson Hole, but none of them have stuck." Adrianna swept her hair off her face with the back of her hand. A group of men in a nearby booth cast admiring glances her way but her friend didn't appear to notice. "What does that tell you?"

"Um, that he just hasn't found the one?"

"Or that he's looking for love in all the wrong places," Adrianna said.

Betsy couldn't help but smile. "Do you *really* have to use the lyrics from a country song to make your point?"

"You have to admit it fits."

While they ate, Betsy wondered if perhaps Adrianna was right. Was Ryan setting his sights on unattainable women? Not that the handsome cowboy-turned-lawyer wasn't a worthy catch himself, but it seemed like the women he chose weren't a good match for him.

Adrianna was a perfect example. Ryan was an outdoors guy who loved winter sports. Once snow started flying, Adrianna considered "being outdoors" as going from a building to her car. Not only that, Ryan was a meat-and-potatoes guy. Adrianna refused to eat anything with a face. The reality was, the two had little in common and Ryan didn't even know it.

This led Betsy to the logical conclusion that Ryan was just mesmerized by Adrianna's beauty. Her friend was beautiful and a wonderful woman. She just wasn't the right woman for him. If Ryan had been around Adrianna for any period of time, he'd have discovered that for himself.

Which meant Betsy didn't need to fear the two being together. In fact, she should be encouraging interaction.

Contemplating that idea, Betsy took a big bite of her slice of pizza and washed it down with a sip of soda. "Ryan told me Tripp should be back in Jackson next week."

"That's what he told me, too." Adrianna said in an offhand tone.

Intrigued, Betsy lifted a brow.

"Tripp called this morning and mentioned he was thinking of relocating. Since I know Jackson Hole so well, he wanted my help and thoughts on various rental possibilities."

"Why would he need your help." Betsy pulled her brows together. "The guy grew up here."

A deep red inched its way up Adrianna's neck.

"It's been a long time since he's been home," Adrianna responded, then promptly changed the subject. "What shall we do tonight? Do you have any thoughts?"

"A movie?"

"We could," Adrianna expelled a sigh. "There's not anything good playing right now."

Wally's Place was an option. Until this moment Betsy had planned to keep Adrianna away from the popular sports bar since she knew Ryan would be there. But perhaps she needed to rethink her strategy. As long as Ryan was into Adrianna, any feelings he might be developing for Betsy wouldn't stand a chance.

He needed to be around Adrianna so he could see just how incompatible they were...

Risky. But deep in her heart, Betsy believed she stood a chance. A good chance. When they were slinging snowballs and insults at each other today, she'd felt a connection. The look she'd seen in his eyes told her he'd felt it, too.

"We could check out Wally's Place." Betsy's casual tone was at odds with her racing heart. "They have a live band tonight."

Adrianna took another bite of pizza, thought for a moment then nodded. "Sounds like fun."

"Would it make you uncomfortable if Ryan were there?" Betsy had to ask. Adrianna didn't appreciate surprises.

"What makes you think he'll be there?"

"From what he's said, he usually goes there on the weekends."

"Ah, now I understand." A knowing look filled Adrianna's eyes. "This is all part of some grand plan, isn't it?"

Betsy simply smiled and let her beautiful friend draw her own conclusions, praying this "grand plan" wouldn't blow up in her face.

～

"Are you sure you don't want to come with me?" Betsy asked with a smile so appealing that Ryan was almost tempted to agree. Emphasis on the word "almost." He didn't like Benedict Campbell enough to go three feet, much less push his way through a crowded room simply to greet the guy.

He lifted his glass of beer. "I'm a little busy."

Betsy rolled her eyes and pushed back her chair. "I guess that means I go by myself."

She pretended to be irritated with Adrianna, who'd also refused her request. Ryan wasn't fooled. It was obvious she'd set it up so that he and her friend could have some time alone together.

He cast a sideways glance. As always, Adrianna looked stunning. Tonight, she wore a green sweater and jeans that hugged her slender curves and made her legs look like they went on forever. The overhead light played off the auburn highlights in her hair. Her copper-colored lipstick emphasized her full lips.

The strange thing was, Ryan felt no urge to kiss her. It must be because they were in a bar. He'd never been into public displays of affection.

"How's the baby business?" he asked when she continued to sit there sipping her martini. If it had been Betsy, she'd have been talking a mile a minute by now. Ryan had to admit that it had taken him a while to get used to the non-stop chatter, but now it felt odd to be sitting in silence.

"It's been surprisingly busy lately." Adrianna turned in her chair to face him. "More women are choosing to have their babies at home. It's a great way for other family members to be a part of the birth. After all, it's a completely natural experience."

Ryan's smile froze on his face. Was she saying that the kids were there for the birth? He couldn't imagine if his mother had wanted him in the room when his little brother was born. He might have had to run away from home. "How nice."

She returned her attention to her martini.

He shifted his gaze to Betsy, who now stood next to the prominent surgeon. Like Adrianna, Betsy wore jeans and a sweater. Unlike her friend, Betsy had a girl-next-door prettiness that made the whole room light up. She was laughing and talking with the doctor as if they were old friends.

"She's really coming out of her shell." Adrianna leaned closer.

Her perfume seemed almost cloying tonight. He sat back. And he didn't appreciate her comment.

"I didn't know Betsy was ever in a shell," he said, rising to her defense. He would have said more but a hand slapped him on the back.

"Why did I know I'd find you here?"

Ryan recognized the voice immediately. He turned in his seat, rising as he did. "I thought you weren't getting into town until next week."

Tripp Randall laughed. "Can't a guy be spontaneous?"

His friend's blonde hair was covered by a ball cap. A hint of a scruff dotted his chin. He cast a curious glance in Adrianna's direction. "Aren't you going to say hello?"

Adrianna rose in one smooth movement, stepped forward and gave their new guest a big hug. "Welcome back to Jackson."

Tripp looped an arm around her neck in a friendly gesture. "Now that's more like it."

Ryan shot him a pointed glance. "If you're expecting a hug from me, you can forget it."

"Mind if I sit?" Before Ryan could answer, Tripp pulled out Betsy's chair and plopped down.

"That spot is taken but I guess you can sit there for now." Ryan slanted a sideways glance at Adrianna. "Unless you prefer it be just you and me?"

Her eyes widened and she looked shocked.

"Just kidding," Ryan told her.

Tripp stared at him and Adrianna. "Are you two a couple?"

"Us? No," Adrianna said, a little too quickly for Ryan's liking, despite the fact that issuing a quick disclaimer had been the first thing that had come to his lips too.

"Actually, I'm here with Betsy," Ryan pointed to where she stood with her hand on the doctor's arm. "She's the one in the blue sweater. I'm also with Adrianna."

"Two women. You're moving up in the world, boy," Tripp said with an easy smile. "I don't believe I know Betsy."

"Keenan McGregor's sister," Ryan said. "I recently hired her as my legal assistant."

"Betsy's a sweetheart," Adrianna said loyally.

For some reason, Ryan didn't want to talk about Betsy with Tripp. He knew his reluctance made no sense. After all, he'd promised Betsy he'd try to get the two of them together. Of course, he reasoned, first he had to make sure his friend was worthy of her. That might take some time.

"How long are you in town?" Ryan asked.

"Depends. Through the holidays, for sure." Tripp's expression turned serious. "Hopefully longer if the job I want comes through. My dad isn't doing well. Since I'm here I'd like to spend as much time with him and my mom as possible."

"I remember you saying he'd been diagnosed with cancer several years ago." Ryan cocked his head. "I thought he'd beaten it."

"That's what we all thought." Tripp pushed back his chair and stood.

"You're leaving?" Adrianna said, sounding panicked.

"Just getting a draw. The waitress looks swamped. Who knows how long it will take her to get to our table." Tripp glanced at Ryan and Adrianna. "Can I get you anything?"

"Another apple martini?" Adrianna said with a smile that Tripp didn't appear to notice.

"I'm okay," Ryan said.

"I'll be back," Tripp said, but instead of turning in the direction of the bar he headed across the room toward Betsy, who'd finally left Benedict's side.

Ryan narrowed his gaze as Tripp approached her. Betsy's tentative smile widened when Tripp pointed in the direction of him and Adrianna. She probably thought he sent the guy to her. As Ryan watched, Tripp crooked his arm. She slid hers through it and sauntered with him toward the bar.

"She doesn't even know him," Ryan said to no one in particular.

"Like I said, our little Betsy is coming into her own." Adrianna laughed. "I knew it would happen."

"What are you talking about?"

"Betsy hasn't always been popular with men," Adrianna said. "That's changed. Lately guys are finally seeing what a great girl she is."

"What guys?" Ryan demanded. Betsy hadn't said word one about other men in her life.

Adrianna shoved her chair back, still managing to look graceful in the process. "I'm going to check out the Ladies room. I'll be back."

Just like that Ryan found himself alone. No Adrianna. No Tripp. Most importantly, no Betsy.

～

Betsy found it easy to converse with Tripp. Perhaps because she didn't care what he thought of her.

He looked different than she remembered, taller, more man than boy. While he didn't make her heart beat even a little faster, with his thick blonde hair, vivid blue eyes and strong features he was an attractive man. Even the scruff on his chin looked good on him.

The tattered jeans and well-worn Henley shirt weren't much to speak of, but perhaps he'd fallen on hard times. She could certainly empathize.

"What brings you back to Jackson Hole?" she asked when they reached the bar.

"I'm out of one job and looking for another." He motioned the bartender over and quickly gave his order. "I have a promising lead here so I'm back for an interview."

"I hope you get the position." Betsy covered his hand that was resting on the bar with hers. "I know how it feels to be out of work and out of money. It's no fun."

He searched her eyes then a tiny smile lifted the corners of his lips. "You have a job now."

"I do." She glanced over her shoulder at Ryan, now sitting alone at the table and waved. "I'm Ryan's legal assistant."

The bartender sat down the drinks and Tripp pulled a twenty from his pocket.

"No." She pushed his crumpled twenty back at him and took one of her own from her purse. She held it out to the portly bald-headed gentleman behind the bar who watched the interchange with an amused smile. "My treat."

The bartender took the money and turned away, already busy with another order.

Tripp tried to push the twenty-dollar bill into her hand but she clenched her fist and shook her head.

"You might not get this job." Betsy hated to be blunt, but Tripp had to be realistic. "I mean, I hope you do, but if you don't, you're going to need every penny to just survive."

His gaze searched her face. His cool blue eyes softened. "Thank you. You're very kind."

"Once you land your job," she said. "You can buy me a drink."

"It's a deal." Tripp slanted a look back at the table. Adrianna had returned and she and Ryan were talking. "He's really obsessed with her."

"Obsessed? What are you talking about?"

"Adrianna. Ryan told me a couple of weeks ago that he thought she was hot." His eyes darkened and Betsy couldn't tell if Tripp was happy about that or not. Perhaps he wanted Adrianna for himself. Or maybe he agreed with her and didn't think the two were a good match.

Betsy swallowed past the lump that had appeared without warning in her throat. "She's as pretty on the inside as she is on the outside."

"How do you feel about her and Harcourt hooking up?"

I hate it, Betsy wanted to cry out, *because he's mine.*

She reminded herself he wasn't hers. Not yet anyway. "If Adrianna and Ryan become a couple, I'll be happy for them."

"Really?" He lifted a brow. "Something in the way you look at him made me think there might be more between you."

"We're friends," Betsy said firmly, hoping to put an end to his fishing expedition.

"Good."

"Why good?"

She felt him rest his hand lightly against her back as they made their way to the table.

"Because I like you, Betsy McGregor," he said. "When I land this new position, I'm going to call and ask you to celebrate with me."

Betsy smiled, knowing he was only teasing. She played along anyway. "Then I'll keep my fingers crossed you get the job."

CHAPTER NINE

Across the room, Ryan's gaze settled on Betsy laughing with Tripp at the bar. A knife twisted in his gut. It had been a long time since he'd felt the sensation flowing through his veins but he recognized it immediately. *Jealousy*.

Surprisingly, it wasn't Adrianna engendering the response, but Betsy. Betsy. With her mile-a-minute mouth just made for kissing. With her snow-ball throwing arm and fabulous cooking skills. With her kind heart and killer monopoly instinct.

He'd watched Adrianna picking her way through the crowd. Seen the admiring glances sent her way. Until recently Ryan had once been one of those guys. Though she was a nice woman, he realized now that his attraction had been superficial, not deep. Certainly not the lasting kind.

When Betsy and Tripp returned to the table, he flashed an easy smile, settling his gaze on Betsy. "What kept you away so long, Bets?"

The childhood nickname, more of an endearment really, felt right on Ryan's tongue.

Even in the dim light, he could see Betsy's cheeks pink.

After staring curiously at Ryan, Tripp handed the drink to Adrianna with a flourish. "Your apple martini, ma'am."

The smile that had been missing from the pretty brunette's lips for most of the evening returned. "I'm not sure about the ma'am part, but thank you, Tripp."

Ryan stood and gestured for Betsy to take his seat, then grabbed a chair from a nearby table and slid it next to hers. When she smiled her thanks, Ryan felt a surge of satisfaction. She hadn't looked at Tripp once since she'd reached the table. When he got his friend alone, Ryan was going to have to make it clear that Betsy was off limits.

Tripp would understand. A real friend never poached on another man's woman.

"You're up to something," Betsy said in a low tone just loud enough for his ears. "I recognize that look in your eyes."

"Ever thought of riding a bull?" Okay so it wasn't a great way to change the direction of the conversation but it was the first thing that popped into his head.

Betsy knew it was noisy in the bar, but had he really asked if she'd ridden a bull? "Ah, no. I lead a rather boring life."

"Our lives are only as boring as we make them." Ryan jumped to his feet and held out his hand. "No time like to present to kick things up a notch."

Betsy accepted his hand and slowly rose to her feet. "Kick what up a notch?"

"Life," Ryan said. "I suspect we've both been sitting on the sidelines playing it safe. It's time to reach out and grab what we want."

Betsy cast a sideways glance at Adrianna, who appeared engrossed in a conversation with Tripp.

"This isn't about her." Ryan leaned close and whispered in her ear. "This is about you."

He stood so near that it seemed a shame not to slide her arm around his waist. She looked into his eyes, not caring what he might see in hers.

Whatever he saw must have pleased him because a slow smile spread across his face. "Are you ready?"

She'd been ready for him for years, but she'd like to hear exactly what he had in mind. She trailed a finger down his shirt-front. If he wanted to live dangerously, she was definitely in the mood. "For what?"

"I'll show you."

Riding a mechanical bull wasn't exactly what Betsy had in mind. The thought of simply *sitting* on the back of a black and white monstrosity scared her spitless.

"This isn't what I thought living dangerously meant," she muttered.

Ryan's hand ran down her leg as he checked her seat. "What did you say, sweetheart?"

She didn't know why he'd started calling her his sweetheart but she liked it. It made her feel connected to him in a very personal way.

"Hey, Ryan." Heidi—or whatever her name was—suddenly appeared holding a bottle of beer loosely between her fingers. "What's up with this? You can't possibly think she's going to stay on."

Betsy lifted her chin. "I can make it eight seconds."

Heidi's peel of laughter felt like a swift slap. "Honey-bunny, I hate to break it to you but this isn't a real bull. Fifteen seconds is what most people do on this one. You'll be lucky to make it two."

"Don't listen to her." Ryan's voice took on a hard edge and his grey eyes were cold as steel. "We're a little busy here."

The woman's gaze drifted from Ryan to Betsy then back to Ryan. "So that's how it is."

"Yes," Ryan said firmly. "That's how it is."

Flipping a strand of long blonde hair over her shoulder, Heidi flounced off.

"I'm going to embarrass you," Betsy said, suddenly miserable.

Surprise flickered in Ryan's eyes.

"Hey, Harcourt." The bored voice of the ride operator interrupted. "This ain't no pony ride. Let me turn it on or get 'er off."

"Shut up, Hank." Ryan didn't even look in the burly man's direction. His gaze remained firmly fixed on Betsy. "Do you want to do this?"

Betsy didn't want to be on the bull. Didn't like having all these people staring at her. But what Ryan said had struck a chord? *Our lives are only as boring as we make them.*

It was as if her life suddenly flashed before her and she realized she'd been living in shades of brown. A careful well-ordered one designed to not draw attention to herself lest anyone compare her with her mother.

But her mother was dead and she was alive. Betsy suddenly realized she didn't want to be brown. She wanted to be red and purple and the vibrant orange that sometimes colored the skies over the Tetons.

"Betsy." Ryan's hand closed over hers. "It's your decision. What do you want to do?"

"Turn it on."

Ryan started having second thoughts when he saw Betsy's legs shaking. This was supposed to be fun. "Are you sure?"

"I'm ready." Betsy gave a decisive nod.

The resolve in her voice reassured him. And her legs had almost stopped shaking. He rested his hand on her shoulder. "Let me give you a couple of pointers."

Ryan went on to explain the importance of squeezing with her thighs, of using her leg muscles to "root" her to the bull. Then he checked her grip and nodded his approval.

"Try to relax your upper body." Even as he said the words, a shiver of unease traveled up his spine. He knew that most riders got rolled off when the ride operator had the bull bow down in front and the rear tipped up. "When the bull leans forward you lean back. Use your free hand for balance. Move with the bull, instead of against it."

He almost made her get off. The fear that she would be hurt hit him with the force of a sledge hammer. But she looked so determined, so brave, he couldn't take the chance away from her.

"I can do this," Betsy vowed, tiny beads of perspiration dotting her brow.

"I know you can." He leaned over and kissed her. Not a peck on the cheek either, but one designed to make her toes curl.

"What was that for?" she asked, her eyes wide and oh-so-beautiful.

"For luck." He winked. "Turn 'er on, Hank."

At first, being on the bull reminded Betsy of riding one of those horses they used to have sitting outside the supermarket. If you put in a quarter, it would go up and down with a gentle rocking motion.

For a second, she felt confident enough to smile. *This isn't so bad.*

Then the front of the bull took a nosedive. Thankfully Betsy had her legs pressed tightly against the sides of the mechanical animal or she'd have been tossed onto the cushioned mat right then. She remembered what Ryan had said and leaned back, waving her hand in the air for balance.

Had that "Yee-Haw," really come from *her* throat?

Just as quickly as the bull lunged forward it rocked back. Betsy kept her upper body fluid and her lower legs tightly gripped.

Calls of "Ride 'em, Betsy" filled the air. Exhilaration fought with fear as the bull gave it everything he had to buck her off.

It was the wildest ride she'd ever been on, but thanks to Ryan's tips, she was prepared. By the time the fifteen seconds was up, Betsy was almost disappointed her time in the spotlight was over.

As the crowd roared its approval, a cowboy she didn't recognize plopped his black Stetson on her head. "Congratulations, cowgirl."

Betsy smiled, feeling as if she'd just been crowned Miss America.

Ryan pulled her into his arms and, with everyone watching, gave her a big kiss. "That's my girl."

Out of the corner of her eye, Betsy saw Heidi turn and meld into the crowd, a sour look on her face.

"You did good, babe," Ryan's eyes looked like liquid silver in the light. "Full fifteen seconds."

"I had fun." Betsy's breath came in short puffs. "I can see why you liked riding bulls. What a rush."

He slung an arm around her shoulders and the crowd parted before them.

Betsy couldn't believe all the congratulations she received, most from people she'd never met. "Adrianna is going to tell me I was crazy to do it," she said, her words running together in excitement. "She doesn't like anything connected with rodeo."

But when they reached the table, it was just Tripp waiting there, a worried expression on his face.

"Where's Adrianna?" Betsy asked, glancing around.

"She didn't feel well," he said. "She ran to the restroom right after you left to ride the bull. She hasn't come back."

Betsy glanced at Ryan.

He smiled reassuringly. "I'm sure she's fine."

"I'm going to check on her anyway."

"If you need anything—" Ryan began, but Betsy had already disappeared.

As Ryan dropped into the chair, he realized his heart had finally settled into a normal rhythm. All those years he'd rode bulls, his mother had rarely come to watch. She'd told him it was too hard for her to sit there and worry. He'd never understood. Until tonight.

Watching Betsy on the back of the mechanical bull had been almost painful. Intellectually he knew if it tossed her, she wouldn't be hurt. Wally's cushioned floor surrounding the bull would see to that. But it wasn't his head that had been stressed seeing her rockin' and a rollin,' but his heart.

While he'd wanted her to stay on so she could experience that thrill, it had taken everything he had not to pull her off and hold her close, hating to take even the slightest chance that she could be hurt.

It hadn't been his legal assistant on the back of that bull. It hadn't been his childhood friend's sister. It had been the woman he loved.

Ryan sat back as the realization washed over him. All the time they'd been spending working and playing, plotting how to get the person they wanted had brought them together in a way that he'd never imagined. Though it sounded corny, he knew Betsy was the one he'd been waiting for his whole life.

Tripp smiled. "You know, even if the hospital doesn't offer me the job, connecting with Betsy made coming back to Jackson worth the trip."

His friend's words and who Tripp was referring to suddenly registered. It sounded as if he was smitten with Betsy.

"I understand you and Adrianna have kept in touch."

It didn't hurt, Ryan thought, to make Tripp aware that he knew where Tripp's interest *really* lie.

"Adrianna and Gayle kept in touch through the years," Tripp said in an off-hand tone. "She's merely a friend."

"Well, Betsy is more than a friend to me." Ryan met the other man's gaze.

Ryan's irritation soared when Tripp laughed. "Don't tell me she's your new flavor-of-the-day? Last time we talked it was Adrianna. Make up your mind, man."

"Betsy is the one—"

Ryan stopped as Betsy and Adrianna walked up. The tall brunette's eyes were watery and her skin unusually pale.

"Adrianna isn't feeling well," Betsy began.

"The stomach flu has been going around the office," Adrianna said with a weak smile. "I'm sorry if I exposed you."

"Do you need help?" Ryan started to rise from his seat.

Betsy waved him back down. "We'll be fine."

She took off the cowboy hat still on her head and handed it to Ryan. "If you could return this to the proper owner, I'd appreciate it."

Ryan took the hat. There were so many things he wanted to say to her, but now wasn't the time or the place. "I'll call you tomorrow."

"It was nice meeting you, Betsy," Tripp said then shifted his gaze to Adrianna. "Take care of yourself."

"We better go, Betsy," Adrianna's pale complexion now looked almost green.

As the two hurried off, Ryan watched them go. The statuesque brunette and her solicitous friend. The woman he thought he'd wanted and the woman who was his perfect match.

After taking her friend home, Betsy had barely opened the door to her apartment when the same bug hit her.

She spent that night and most of Saturday alternating between the bedroom and the bathroom. Puffy watched her from the hall with worried eyes. When Betsy awakened Sunday morning to the ringing of her phone, she realized that for the first time in almost thirty-six hours her stomach felt normal.

She fumbled for the phone she'd flung onto the beside-stand sometime yesterday. "Hello."

"I'm picking you up for church in forty-five minutes."

Betsy pulled the phone from her ears and stared at it. "Who is this?"

"Who do you think it is? Ryan."

"Good morning, Ryan." He'd called several times yesterday but she'd been in no shape to talk to anyone.

"Why didn't you return my calls?"

"I was, ah, incapacitated with the same bug that hit Adrianna." Betsy plumped up several pillows and sat up in bed. "I'm better now."

"You should have told me." Concern filled his voice. "I'd have brought you over some chicken soup or something."

"Trust me, you wouldn't have wanted to be here."

"I could have taken care of you," he insisted. "Or at the least kept Puffy out of your hair."

Betsy glanced at the small red Pomeranian. Other than demanding to be fed and taken outside on schedule, the dog hadn't been much trouble. "Puffy was no problem."

"Well, consider this fair warning. Next time you don't answer my calls, I'm coming over," he said. "I don't like it that you were home all alone and sick."

Her heart rose to her throat. There he went again, confusing her by acting as if he truly cared. "Well, I'm better now."

"Good. I'll have the truck nice and warm for you."

Where had he said he wanted to take her? Ah, yes, to church.

"I don't attend Sunday services." Betsy had gone a couple of times with friends when she'd been small. Once she realized God really didn't answer prayers she hadn't been back.

"It'll be fun." He spoke with such enthusiasm she found herself believing him. "It's casual so you don't need to dress up. Afterwards we'll go with everyone for breakfast at The Coffee Pot. They have bland things—like oatmeal--on the menu, too so you should be able to find something to eat."

Betsy was familiar with the café in downtown Jackson. It was known for its hearty country-style breakfast fare. She wondered who Ryan was referring to when he said 'everyone?' She knew church wasn't on Adrianna's agenda. "Will Tripp be there?"

Silence filled the other end of the line. "Probably not. Does that make the difference?"

"No," she said, surprised by the edge to his voice. "I was simply curious who 'everyone' was?"

"It varies from week to week," Ryan informed her. "Usually Lexi and Nick Delacourt, David and July Wahl, Travis and Mary Karen Fisher and Cole and Meg. If they're in town, Derek and Rachel Rossi usually show up, too, as well as a few others."

Although Betsy was acquainted with everyone that Ryan mentioned, she didn't run in their social circle. Of course, there was no reason she couldn't get to know them better. And perhaps get to know Ryan better in the process? After all, hadn't someone once said that to know a man, you just need look at his friends? "How long do I have to get ready?"

"Forty minutes."

Betsy swung her legs to the side of the bed and stood, already eyeing her closet. "Okay. And Ryan?"

"Yes."

"Thanks."

"For what?"

"For caring that I was sick and offering to come over." She kept her thanks simple, not wanting to be maudlin. "I haven't had anyone who cared for a long time."

"Well," he said. "Get used to it. Now you do."

CHAPTER TEN

Sitting beside Ryan in church felt oddly intimate. When he opened the book in his hand for the next song, Betsy smiled. After the opening hymn she'd discovered Ryan had a surprisingly good voice and that their voices blended together as if they'd been singing harmony their whole lives.

She wasn't so much conscious of the words as she was the beautiful melody. Life was certainly strange. When Betsy had tumbled into bed last night, she'd never thought she'd be sitting in a church this morning.

As they sat down Ryan took the book from her hand, his fingers brushing against hers, lingering for an extra beat. Electricity traveled up her arm. He must have felt it too because his eyes met hers. For a second she thought he might kiss her right then and there. If that wasn't shocking enough, she had a feeling she'd have let him.

Someone read some Scripture, but Betsy scarcely noticed. It was as if there was a bubble around her and Ryan and they were the only two in the room. When he reached over and took her hand, she curled her fingers through his and expelled a happy sigh.

Betsy knew she should ask why he hadn't mentioned inviting Adrianna, but she didn't want to spoil her fantasy. For just this morning she wanted to pretend that Ryan wanted her and no one else.

"Grace is something needed but not deserved," the minister intoned.

The sermon this morning appeared to be centered around forgiveness. It was a topic Betsy preferred not to think about. Those who didn't know her relationship with her mother, who didn't know all she'd endured growing up, often spouted the forgiveness talk. Betsy was having none of it today.

She'd heard all about forgiveness setting you free, but she already felt free. How could she forgive a woman who'd never asked for her forgiveness? Who'd gone her merry way through life, hurting all those around her? Who'd even at the time of her death been in a destructive mode?

Betsy hated that the preacher had a voice that was hard to ignore. She did her best, concentrating on the feel of her hand in Ryan's, on his muscular thigh pressed up against her in the packed pew.

Dress casually, Ryan had said. Thankfully she hadn't tossed on a pair of jeans like she'd considered when she'd hopped out of her super quick shower. She'd chosen a wrap-around tweed dress with brown boots and tights. When Ryan whistled, in that moment she'd felt beautiful.

He was actually the one who was beautiful in his dark pants and grey sweater. The way he smelled…so good she couldn't stop thinking of that time he'd crawled under her covers. If she had him there now, she'd make sure they did a whole lot more than just talk.

"Time to stand." Ryan tugged her to her feet.

She rose, her heart pumping hard and fast, unable to let go of the image of him in her bed, a visual that seemed stuck in her consciousness.

The minister offered a benediction. When he quit speaking Betsy realized she'd sat through her first church service in over five years. Other than the forgiveness part, it had been bearable. Ryan kept hold of her hand as they exited the pew. It was then that the hoard descended.

Okay, so maybe it wasn't a *hoard*. But close. Ryan's friends seemed to come out from the woodwork.

"When did you and Ryan start dating?" Mary Karen Fisher had pulled her blonde hair back in a bouncy ponytail, making her look more like a college coed than a mother of five.

Betsy had always liked Mary Karen. She was as upbeat and friendly now as she'd been back in high school. Which was amazing considering she had five small children at home, four of them boys.

"We're not actually—" Betsy began.

"Just started," Ryan said before she could finish.

"You're a good match for him." Lexi Delacourt, a prominent social worker in Jackson Hole, nodded her approval.

"What makes you think that?" Betsy asked.

"Call me for drinks sometime." Lexi winked. "I'll tell you why."

"Lexi," Meg Lassiter called out. "We're heading over to The Coffee Pot to get a table."

"You guys are coming, aren't you?" Mary Karen asked.

Ryan placed a hand on Betsy's shoulder. "We'll be there."

The two of them slowly strolled out of church. The sky overhead was a bright blue and the sun shone warm against her face. Ryan was telling her a story about when Lexi's husband came to Jackson Hole, got caught in an avalanche while skiing the back country and lost his memory.

The tale was so unbelievable that she wondered if Ryan made it up. Or maybe this was *all* a dream. It felt like one. Ryan calling her for a date. Being so attentive.

She looped her arm through his. If this was a dream, she was going to enjoy every minute of it.

~

"Oh no," Betsy said when they drew close to The Coffee Pot. "There's a line."

"No worries." Ryan smiled and edged his way through the crowd, then led her through the maze of tables to a large one in the back. "See. Cole and Meg got the table."

Betsy recognized another one of the couples already seated. Joel Dennes was a prominent contractor in town. His wife, Kate, was a pediatrician. She was also one of Ryan's former girlfriends.

Awkward, Betsy thought to herself as Ryan held out her chair seating her next to the couple. After introducing her to Joel and Kate, he smiled. "I hear congratulations are in order."

Betsy tilted her head.

"We're having a baby." Kate slipped her hand through her husband's arm.

"Congrats from me, too," Betsy said. "When are you due?"

"The middle of June." Kate's face lit up like a Christmas tree. "Our daughter Chloe is thrilled. She said she doesn't need any other presents. Knowing she'll soon have a brother or sister is present enough."

"We know when it comes time to unwrap gifts, she'll want something more under the tree," Joel said with an indulgent smile.

Once it got going, the conversation flowed easily. Betsy had seen Kate around but she'd always seemed a bit stand-offish. Today she discovered that Kate was as nice as she was pretty. Dark brown hair with big hazel eyes and a curvy yet lithe figure, Betsy felt like an ugly country mouse sitting next to a pretty city one.

Ryan was in his element, laughing and joking with his friends. Although everyone was friendly, Betsy held back, not sure of her place in this group, not wanting to be too bold.

The man at her side would have none of it. Ryan skillfully

drew her into the conversation, first by making them aware that she was Keenan's sister, then telling all her secrets. From her bull-riding talent to her skill with snowballs.

"You should come out to our house sometime." Kate paused for a moment as the waitress placed plates of food—and her bowl of oatmeal—on the table. "We could build a fort or have a snowball fight. Chloe would love it."

"Count us in," Mary Karen leaned across the table. "As long as we can bring the boys."

Mary Karen's oldest set of twins were two boys who made Dennis the Menace look like a choir boy.

"If we play, we get Betsy on our team," her husband Travis announced.

"What about me?" Ryan pretended to be outraged.

"You already said how good she was," Mary Karen said in a matter-of-fact tone. "Naturally we took that to mean she can take you out."

"Yep," he said, bringing her hand to his lips and kissing it. "She can take me out, anywhere, anytime."

Betsy looked him in the eyes and wondered if he'd say the same thing if Adrianna was sitting beside him. She prayed he was sincere. If he wasn't, she was in trouble. Because she was falling more deeply in love with him by the second.

"Have you slept with him yet?"

"Adrianna, shush," Betsy hissed. "Someone might hear you."

The two women had spent the morning checking out the current exhibit at the National Museum of Wildlife Art then stayed to grab some lunch at the Red Sage Café, located inside the building.

Adrianna glanced around the empty café. "There's no one here. Everyone is out Christmas shopping or skiing."

"I don't feel comfortable discussing my personal life in such a public venue." Betsy kept her voice low.

Although Jackson Hole held almost twenty thousand people, it was also a close-knit community. The last thing she wanted to do was to get some gossip going about her and Ryan.

"Okay, how about if I speak in a whisper?" Adrianna grinned, her voice as loud as before. "Then will you tell me your secrets?"

"There's nothing to tell," Betsy said. "We're only friends."

Adrianna took a bite of her tuna pita. "You really expect me to believe that? I saw the way he looked at you last Friday at Wally's."

"I've seen the way he looks at *you*." Betsy took a sip of her ice tea, hoping that Adrianna would drop this line of questioning, but knowing she wouldn't. "I don't appeal to him in that way."

Adrianna waved away the comment. She chewed thoughtfully. "Perhaps he doesn't want to push you."

Or maybe he's in love with you.

The thought rose unbidden from the deepest recesses of Betsy's subconscious. Ryan had made it clear he liked being with her, yet he *had* originally enlisted her to help him win over Adrianna. He'd also told Tripp that it was Adrianna he wanted.

Was spending time with her part of a plan to make Adrianna jealous? Or had he simply decided to settle for second best?

Betsy sighed. "Ryan and I are friends, Anna. I've told you that many times."

"Still not believing it."

That's because so far Betsy knew she hadn't been all that convincing. "I think Tripp is going to ask me out."

Adrianna's eyes widened and she straightened in her seat. "Are you going to go?"

"Of course," Betsy said with what she hoped was a convincing smile. "Why wouldn't I?"

～

Betsy picked up her purse, ready to head out the door when Ryan called to her from his office. She sighed and sat down her bag on her desk, hoping this wouldn't be another invitation to stay late.

All week Ryan had been consumed by a case scheduled for court next week. Every night he'd asked her to work late. The first time it had happened she'd thought he had something more personal in mind. But when he'd pulled out his case notes and started to talk, her hopes of a more intimate evening sank like a lead balloon. It had been the same story every night since.

By the time they finished it was usually close to ten and she'd gone home exhausted. Too tired to even trim her Christmas tree. It still sat in her living room, in water, begging for decorations. She'd thought about asking Ryan if he wanted to come over this weekend to help but decided against it.

She'd started to wonder if the connection she'd felt between them had been all in her head. That's why when Tripp had called, told her he'd gotten the job and offered to take her out to dinner to celebrate, she'd said yes.

"You need something?" Betsy asked, stopping in the doorway to Ryan's adjoining office.

He looked up and she saw the lines of fatigue around his eyes. Putting down his mouse, he sat back in the leather-and-cowhide desk chair. "We've both put in a lot of hours this week. I'd like to take you out for dinner as a token of my appreciation."

A token of his appreciation. The sentiment was sweet but it hit Betsy wrong. Like he felt forced to take her out.

"Thanks for the kind offer," she said in as pleasant of a tone as she could muster through gritted teeth. "I already have plans for dinner."

"Oh, are you and Adrianna getting together?"

Now he was really starting to get on her nerves. Granted, some of her less-than-good mood was probably because she was tired, but did he really think she didn't have any other options than dinner with a girlfriend?

"Actually, no. Tripp is taking me out to dinner."

Ryan pushed back his chair and stood. His brows pulled together. "Tripp Randall asked you out?"

Anger shot up Ryan's spine. After that night at Wally's Place, he'd told Tripp he was interested in Betsy and to back off. Of course, come to think of it, Tripp hadn't agreed. His friend had just laughed and asked if Betsy was Ryan's flavor-of-the day?

When he'd asked Tripp what he meant by that crack, Tripp had said they both knew his infatuation with Betsy wouldn't last. After all, barely two weeks ago he'd told Tripp he was sure Adrianna was 'the one.'

It pissed Ryan off to know that Tripp was right about him, or rather former Ryan. Though he knew his friend hadn't meant to hit a nerve, he had. For a few seconds all Ryan could think was he sounded a whole lot like his Uncle Jed.

Uncle Jed had three ex-wives and a girlfriend young enough to be his daughter. That wasn't the kind of life Ryan wanted for himself. He wanted a lasting relationship like his parents had. He wanted to marry and have children. He wanted that life with Betsy.

Regardless of what Tripp implied, Betsy was different than the others.

You thought Adrianna was different too, a little voice whispered in his head. He immediately silenced it and focused on the conversation at hand.

"Is there anything else?" Betsy asked.

She hadn't really answered his question but, from the look on her face, it wouldn't be safe to ask again. But he'd be damned if he'd let Tripp monopolize her weekend.

"Joel called and asked if we wanted to come out for some fun-in-the-snow at their place tomorrow."

"You mean he called and invited *you*."

"Yes, but he specifically mentioned wanting you to come."

Ryan had planned on talking to her about those plans over dinner tonight. Those plans had gone up in smoke.

Because she was having dinner with Tripp.

Ryan took a deep breath and forced a smile. "It should be fun. Afterwards I thought we might decorate your tree, if you haven't decorated it already, that is."

"When would I have time to trim the tree?" Her expression softened. "My boss is a real slave-driver and I spend all my time at work."

Hope rose in his chest. "So you'll do it?"

"Sure," she said. "Sounds like fun."

"I can pick you—"

"Call me tomorrow," she said before he could finish. "I've got to run."

"Okay," he said. "I'll call you in the morning."

"Not too early," she said as she headed toward the front door. "I may be out late."

CHAPTER ELEVEN

By the time Ryan called her the next morning at ten and told her they were expected for lunch at noon, Betsy had to scramble to get ready.

She'd had fun with Tripp. He'd taken her to the Spring Gulch Country Club for a night of dinner and dancing. When he told her to dress up, she thought he'd been kidding. Just in case, she pulled on a little black dress she'd bought last year on clearance.

When he'd shown up wearing a suit and tie, she was glad she'd taken the time. Yet she worried about the cost of the meal and the price of the bottle of wine he'd ordered after he announced he was the new hospital administrator at Jackson Hole Memorial. Apparently, Mr. Stromburg was retiring and they'd picked Tripp to fill his shoes. He'd come to Jackson Hole to meet with the Hospital Board before they confirmed the offer.

She told him that while it was good that he had gotten a job, there could still be cash flow problems while waiting for that first check. He'd simply smiled.

They'd laughed and talked and danced. She'd had fun but when he put his arms around her while they were dancing, she couldn't help but wish it were Ryan holding her tight.

The doorbell rang as Betsy was tying her Caribou snow boots. If she and Ryan were going to play in the snow, she was prepared. Flannel lined pants, ski sweater with silk underwear, Eskimo parka and pink plaid aviator hat.

She'd told Tripp last night about her plans. When she'd mentioned she was planning on wearing her aviator's cap with the fur inside, he'd laughed. He'd told her if he could wrangle an invitation, he'd go simply to see her in that hat.

The doorbell rang again.

"Coming," she called out.

Puffy ran ahead barking her own greeting.

Betsy hurried to the door and flung it open. Her heart flip-flopped when she saw Ryan. "Good morning."

His navy ski coat made his eyes look more blue than grey and the smile on his face was enough to melt her heart. He held out a cup to her.

"What's this?" She took the cup from his hands and waved him inside.

"Cappuccino. I know it's your favorite and I thought it'd get your Saturday morning off to a good start."

Betsy tilted her head when she saw his hands were now empty. "You didn't get one for yourself?"

"I drank mine on the way over."

Betsy took a sip. "It's delicious."

"That good, eh?"

"Here." She held out the cup to him. "Try it."

He glanced down where her lips had once been and she immediately regretted her impulsive gesture.

"I'm so sorry. Take off the lid—"

His lips closed on the same spot where hers had been only moments before. "It *is* good." His gaze never left hers. "I don't mind drinking after you. After all, we've kissed. How is this different?"

"We kissed a long time ago." Betsy stopped herself from admitting that she knew exactly how many days it had been since he'd last kissed her. "It scarcely counts."

"I can remedy that."

Before she knew what was happening, he'd placed the cup on the side table near the front door and tugged her to him. Betsy told herself not to fall under his spell, but an invisible web had already begun to weave around her, pulling her in.

He tilted her chin up with a curved finger before his mouth closed over hers. His kiss was sweet and slow, exquisitely gentle and achingly tender.

The momentary thought that she should pull away vanished as she gave into the moment, to the delicious sensations streaming through her body.

His tongue swept across her lips and she opened her mouth to him. A smoldering heat flared through her, a sensation she didn't bother to fight.

"Oh, Bets." His voice was a husky caress.

His hand slid under her sweater, beneath the silky undergarment. Red flags popped up in her head. She ignored them.

His long fingers lifted and supported her yielding flesh as his thumbs brushed across the tight points of her nipples. All the while he continued to kiss her.

Then a knock sounded at her door.

She stiffened.

"Ignore it," he murmured.

When three more quick knocks sounded at the door Betsy knew the unexpected visitor wasn't going away. "It's Mr. Marstand from next door. That's his signal. He knows I'm home."

With obvious reluctance, Ryan dropped his hands to his sides and took a step back.

Betsy adjusted her sweater and hurried to open the door. Her elderly neighbor stood shivering in a light jacket.

Stepping aside Betsy motioned him inside. "Mr. Marstand, you need a heavier coat."

The older gentleman wasn't much taller than Betsy with a mop of unruly white hair and skin pulled taut over his bones. His mustache needed trimming. But his dark eyes were bright and missed nothing.

"I'm only shivering because it took you so long to open the door." Ralph Marstand's eyes settled on Ryan.

After pushing the front door shut, Betsy turned and hurried to the sofa. She grabbed a cotton throw and wrapped it around the man then gestured to the sofa. "Take a seat," she said. "I'll brew you up a nice cup of tea."

Ryan was all about being hospitable but they were expected at Cole and Meg's for lunch. He tried to catch Betsy's eye but she was too focused on the old man.

He dropped in a chair opposite the man and Puffy immediately jumped into his lap. Ryan thought about pushing the Pom off but Mr. Marstand was staring.

"How long have you known Betsy?" the old man asked.

It had been years since Ryan had dated a girl, rather than a woman. He remembered being back in high school and having to be interviewed by their father before his date could leave the house. "Pretty much all her life. I'm a friend of her brother Keenan."

"The one who's in prison?"

"I'm sure Betsy's told you that Keenan is innocent." Without realizing what he was doing Ryan stroked Puffy's soft fur. To his surprise, instead of growling or baring her teeth, the puffball licked his hand.

"You spent the night."

"What?"

"You heard me." The older man's eyes were filled with disapproval.

"I just got here." Ryan paused. Had Betsy had an overnight

guest? Could Tripp have... Nah, Betsy was too smart to succumb to Tripp's charm. But then she *had* sounded sleepy when he'd called, like he'd awakened her. The question was, who else had he awakened?

"Did you see a car parked over here last night?" Ryan fought to keep his tone casual and off-hand.

Before the old man could answer, Betsy swept into the room with a tray in her hand and three cups of steaming tea. She smiled at the two men and placed the tray on the coffee table. "I heard you chatting in the kitchen. What were you talking about?"

"He wanted to know if the guy who picked you up last night-- the tall blonde one--spent the night." Mr. Marstand picked up one of the mugs and took a sip.

"What?" Betsy's eyes narrowed. "How dare you?"

Puffy hopped off his lap as if it were a sinking ship.

"Nonono," Ryan said. "You misunderstand. He was interrogating me—"

"I asked you a few simple questions," Mr. Marstand said with great indignation. "Since when is it a crime to be friendly?"

"He was the one who asked if I'd spent the night."

"I don't recall that part." The old man tapped his head with a forefinger. "Then again, my memory isn't what it used to be."

Betsy gave Marstand an understanding smile.

Ryan wanted to slug him.

"Did you ask Mr. Marstand if Tripp spent the night?" Betsy pinned him with her gaze.

"I did not," Ryan said.

"You asked if there was a car parked here overnight," Mr. Marstand said pointedly.

Great. The old guy chose now to regain his memory.

Betsy met Ryan's gaze. "Is that true?"

A trickle of sweat trailed down Ryan's back. Asking that question hadn't been one of his finer moments, but lying would only make it worse. "Marstand, er Mr. Marstand, implied I'd spent the night. I knew I hadn't so I asked him if there'd been a car parked here overnight."

Betsy shifted her gaze to the old man.

The white-haired man shrugged. "Could have happened that way."

To Ryan's surprise, Betsy laughed. "What am I going to do with you two?"

"Tell us about your date last night," the old man said.

Ryan sloshed a bit of tea onto his hand. Just when he was starting to think the geezer wasn't so bad, he went and did this. Then Ryan realized, perhaps the man had done him a favor. After all, it would have been tacky for him to pump Betsy about details of her date with Tripp. This way he wouldn't have to, the old guy would do it for him.

He shot Mr. Marstand an encouraging smile.

Betsy picked up her cup of tea. "His name is Tripp Randall," she said, taking a sip. "Like Ryan, he was a high school friend of my brother's."

"Randall?" Mr. Marstand rubbed the grey stubble on his chin. "Is he related to Franklin Randall who owns Spring Gulch Land and Cattle?"

"Isn't that the big cutting horse and cattle ranch south of Jackson?" Betsy asked.

"That's his dad's place," Ryan confirmed.

Betsy pulled her brows together as if trying to sort everything out. "Tripp is rich?"

A lump the size of a large boulder settled in the pit of Ryan's stomach. To someone from Betsy's background, heck to almost anyone, Tripp's wealth would be very appealing.

"You don't look very happy, punkin'." Mr. Marstand's worried gaze settled on Betsy. "Something troubling you?"

"Yes, something's wrong," Betsy said. "I paid for Tripp's drink at the bar last weekend because I thought he was in dire straits. I chastised him for buying a bottle of wine last night. I feel like a fool. That man definitely owes me an explanation."

The minute she arrived with Ryan at Joel and Kate's new home in the mountains surrounding Jackson, Betsy knew her day was going to get even more interesting. Standing inside the foyer, nursing a tall glass of hot apple cider was Tripp Randall.

He lifted a hand in a semblance of a greeting and cast a pointed glance at her head.

Betsy held up her aviator hat but when he motioned for her to put it on, she shook her head. She was still angry about his deception.

"We have a buffet table set up in the Great Room," Kate said with a welcoming smile. "Help yourself."

Joel held out his hand and Betsy couldn't think of any reason not to give him her coat. Except she had on pants with flannel lining that made her butt look big and her ski sweater had a stripe across the chest. 'nuff said.

With Ryan's help, she shrugged out of her bulky parka, placing it in Joel's outstretched hands. The second Ryan handed Joel his coat, he placed his hand against the small of Betsy's back. The solicitude confused her. Adrianna wasn't here today. There was no reason for Ryan to act this way—

Tripp.

Betsy had forgotten that Ryan thought she had the hots for the rich hospital administrator. Had he made sure Tripp was invited today? But was that before or after he'd kissed her so ardently?

"Tripp." Ryan's smile didn't quite reach his eyes. "I didn't expect to see you here today."

The man's gaze settled on Betsy and his lips lifted in a slight smile. "I heard there was a party and invited myself."

"Don't let him feed you a line," Joel said after hanging up the coats. "Any son of Franklin Randall is always welcome in my home."

"You know Frank?" Ryan asked.

It seemed a valid question to Betsy, since Joel had only moved to Jackson Hole several years earlier from Montana.

"Building another guesthouse on his property was my first big job when I expanded my business to Jackson Hole," Joel said, as they walked down the hall to the Great Room at the back of the large log home.

Joel glanced at Betsy and Ryan. "I understand you're all old friends."

"Ryan and I go back to high school days," Tripp said. "Betsy and I are relatively new friends. Of course, I've known her brother Keenan all my life."

"Does your brother live in Jackson Hole?" Joel asked.

"He lives in Rawlins." It wasn't as if it was a big secret that Keenan was in prison, but Betsy didn't feel like answering a lot of questions right now.

"Betsy and I went to the Spring Gulch Country Club for dinner last night," Tripp said. "I'd forgotten how good the food is there."

She breathed a sigh of relief when the conversation moved to the newly revised menu at the Country Club and off her brother. She didn't have much to add. Last night had been her first visit to the Country Club. Before her eyes had been open to the possibilities she'd considered upscale dining to be dinner at Perfect Pizza, where you ordered at the counter but they brought the food to your table.

The doorbell rang and Joel smiled. "Help yourself to some food," he said. "I think you probably know almost everyone here. If not, introduce yourselves. Once everyone has eaten, we'll head outside."

Betsy stared at the group of people, many the same as she'd

met in church. Some familiar. Some not at all. Children were everywhere, preteens to little toddlers. The room buzzed with conversation and laughter.

Though Betsy considered herself to be fairly outgoing, she was suddenly overcome with the realization that she didn't belong here. These were the beautiful people of Jackson Hole, the doctors, the lawyers, the elite. She was a legal assistant. A woman whose mother had been a show girl in Las Vegas before turning to the bottle.

Her breath came short and shallow as panic edged its fingers up her spine. "I'm going to run to the restroom and wash my hands," she said to no one in particular, though both Ryan and Tripp were nearby. "I'll be back."

She asked directions from a friendly blonde woman, who introduced herself as Rachel Rossi and the curly-haired adolescent beside her as her daughter Mickie, then headed off the way they pointed.

Betsy hadn't gone far when she ran into Kate, looking like she could have stepped off a cover of an 'outdoor fun' spread in a magazine. Her classic black ski pants looked like they had been made for her and the cable-knit sweater in a burnt orange didn't look at all bulky.

"It's good to see you again," Kate said with a warmth that surprised her.

Betsy shifted from one foot to the other as a large peel of laughter sounded from the other room.

"If my ears aren't deceiving me that's Mary Karen Fisher." Kate smiled. "I swear the woman has never met a stranger. I wish I were more like her."

Betsy tilted her head; not sure she'd heard correctly. "You're very social."

"Thank you for that." Kate smiled. "The truth is I'm actually quite shy. The first time I went for breakfast with Joel at The

Coffee Pot and saw everyone sitting there, I wanted to turn on my heel and walk the other way…quickly."

The tension in Betsy's shoulders eased. "I had the same feeling when I walked into your living room. I told Ryan and Tripp that I wanted to go wash my hands but it was an excuse. I needed to collect my thoughts."

"A few deep breaths don't hurt either." Kate chuckled. "How about I walk in with you? It'll make it easier for both of us."

"Sounds good." When Kate started to turn in the direction of the Great Room, Betsy placed a hand on her arm. "Can I ask you something first?"

"Of course. You can ask me anything."

"You and Ryan dated."

"We did." A hint of wariness crept into Kate's gaze. "Right before Joel and I got together."

"What happened?" Betsy asked before it hit her that might be too personal of a question. "If you don't mind my asking that is…"

"Ryan is a nice guy." Kate's fondness for the attorney was evident in her gaze. "We had fun together. I still consider him a good friend. But the spark, the sizzle, for whatever reason it just wasn't there. Then I met Joel and I knew it was him. He was the one for me."

"Tripp told me that Ryan tends to run hot then cold with women."

"I bet he also told you that when things go south, you should think of him."

"I told him that Ryan and I are simply friends."

"Oh, sweetie, I'm sure he didn't believe that any more than I do." Kate's eyes softened. "I've seen the way you look at him."

"Oh God, is it that obvious?" Betsy brought her hands to her suddenly hot face.

"No. Of course not," Kate said reassuringly. "But you do like Ryan?"

Betsy settled for a nod.

"If he wants to date you, then I'd give it a shot." Kate smiled. "Think of it this way; what's the worst that could happen?"

He could break my heart, Betsy thought to herself, *shatter it into a million little pieces and I'd never be able to put it together again.*

"You're right," Betsy said. "I don't have anything to lose."

CHAPTER TWELVE

Betsy didn't see Ryan when she and Kate returned to the Great Room but Tripp was hanging out by a tall Fiscus tree decorated in bright orange pumpkin lights.

"Oh my," Betsy said.

"I know they're garish, but my daughter Chloe loves them," Kate said.

"It's not that," Betsy mumbled.

"Then what is…" Kate stopped then smiled. "Looks like you have your pick of men this evening."

"When it rains it pours." Betsy could feel the medallion in the pocket of her pants. She wasn't sure why she'd brought it. Courage, perhaps?

"Look, if you want, we can hang out—"

"Thank you, but as the hostess I know you have a lot to do." Betsy offered a reassuring smile. "I'll be just fine."

Kate searched her eyes. "Sure?"

"Positive." Betsy laid a hand on Kate's arm. "I feel so much better after talking to you. Like I'm in the home of a friend."

"That's because you are," Kate said. "I hope you and I can become good friends."

"Mo-om." A thin preteen girl who was a younger version of Kate motioned to her. "You're needed in the kitchen."

"Go," Betsy said. "I'm fine."

Kate gave Betsy's arm a companionable squeeze. "Well, if you need me, you know where to find me."

What I need, Betsy thought, *is a good stiff drink. Or perhaps a bubble bath.* She'd always done some of her best thinking when up to her neck in fragrant suds.

"Glass of wine, my dear?"

Betsy looked up to find Tripp standing beside her, a glass of white wine in one hand and a glass of red in the other.

"Which one is for me?" she asked.

"Whichever one you like," he said, shooting her a smile that showed off a mouthful of straight, white teeth. "I hedged my bets by getting one of each."

"Aren't you the clever one?" She took the burgundy and glanced around the room. "Where's Ryan?"

"Does it matter where—?"

"Of course, it matters." Ryan suddenly appeared beside her. "I was looking for you."

Betsy knew it was crazy but she felt better just having him there. "I ran into Kate and we got to talking."

"I think you two could be really good friends," he said.

"You would know," Tripp said. "You dated her for—"

"It's been great seeing you, Tripp, but Betsy and I have some things we need to discuss. In private." Ryan's gaze met Tripp's. There was something in his stance, in the tilt of his jaw that said the topic wasn't up for discussion.

"See you later, Betsy," Tripp said pointedly before he walked away.

Ryan held out his hand. "Take a walk with me."

Betsy glanced around. "Won't it be rude to take off? We just got here."

Ryan chuckled. "I don't mean leave, just walk around the

house with me."

"Oh." Betsy attempted a laugh. "You must think I'm stupid."

She knew it was because she was nervous. Oh, who was she kidding? It was Ryan. Whenever he was near he made her feel like an awkward school girl who barely knew her own name.

"There are a lot of things I think when I look at you." He tucked a strand of hair behind her ear. "Never stupid."

She didn't know what to say so she glanced around the room. "Look, Benedict Campbell is here."

Ryan muttered something. It almost sounded like a curse, but that couldn't be right. She noticed Ben was standing by himself. "Maybe we should go over and say hello."

"Later," Ryan said. "Much later."

He took her arm and steered her toward the stairs. "Have you seen the upstairs?"

"We can't go upstairs," Betsy hissed, digging in her heels.

"Joel," Ryan called out as their host walked past. "I want to show Betsy the upstairs. Do you mind?"

Something unspoken passed between the two men. Joel smiled. "Not at all."

"I won't touch anything," Betsy said.

"No worries," Joel said.

"C'mon." Out of the corner of one eye, Ryan saw Benedict headed their way. It had been hard enough to get Betsy away from Tripp. Ben wouldn't be so easily dismissed.

Ryan tugged on Betsy's hand. This time she came willingly. They climbed the stairs together and stopped. At the far end of the hall was an alcove with a loveseat. "This way."

When they reached the loveseat, he sat and pulled her down next to him. He took the wine glass she held clutched in one hand and sat it on the side table next to the small sofa.

"What's going on, Ryan?" Betsy's brows were pulled together and her eyes were clearly puzzled. "Why did you bring me up here? Were you, are you ashamed of me?"

She looked so miserable that anger rose inside him. Betsy was a wonderful, beautiful woman. He'd like to get his hands on the man or men that had caused this insecurity. "You look lovely. I brought you up here because I wanted to be alone with you. Not with you and Tripp. Or you and Benedict."

"You wanted to be alone with me? That's why we're here?"

"Do you mind?" Without realizing what he was doing, Ryan held his breath.

"I like being with you." She smiled and ducked her head as if she'd said something intensely personal.

Unless he was simply reading too much into her words, it sounded as if she'd said she didn't mind him pulling her away from Tripp and Benedict. As if she wanted to be alone with him as much as he wanted to be alone with her. The thought gave him courage.

"I like being with you, too. That's what I wanted to talk to you about." Ryan took a deep breath. "I want us to date for real. Not this pretend stuff."

Betsy inhaled sharply but her expression gave nothing away. "Really?"

This was her reaction? *Really.* A response that told him absolutely nothing. He comforted himself that at least she hadn't said no.

"I realize you like Tripp, but I get the feeling you like me, too." He forced himself to breathe past the tightness in his chest. "I'd like to give us a chance."

As she sat there, saying nothing, he realized that in his perfect world, she'd have flung her arms around his neck and cried out yes, yes, yes. It didn't appear that was going to happen. He waited a few more seconds—which seemed an eternity—then spoke. "What are you thinking?"

"What about Adrianna?"

"What about her?"

"You liked her. You thought she was," Betsy paused and swallowed hard, "the one."

"I was mistaken." Ryan couldn't believe he'd ever thought he and Adrianna would be a good match. But he couldn't say that to Betsy. She was her friend and might think he was dissing the woman.

"Would you date me? For real?"

"Yes," she said. "I'd—I'd like that."

"You would?" Dear God, was that a quiver in his voice?

She jerked her head downward, a short quick nod.

He wrapped his arms around her and pulled her close. "That makes me happy."

"It makes me happy, too," she said, her breath warm against her neck.

He kissed her gently, sweetly, with all the love in his heart.

"This is so unreal," she murmured arching her neck back giving him access to the sensitive skin behind her ear. "I've never—"

She moaned as he sucked on her ear lobe and he missed whatever she had said. He could have let it go but he was curious.

"You've never what?" he asked.

"I've never dated two men at once before."

Ryan jerked back as the words registered. "Two men? What are you talking about?"

"You and Tripp." Betsy snuggled against him. "Before it would have just been him that was *really* interested. You and I were just pretending."

"Tripp isn't interested." He couldn't be, Ryan thought. He'd made it clear to his friend that he needed to back off.

Betsy pushed away his hands and sat up, a strange look on her face. "What do you mean by that?"

Take a second, Ryan's rational part urged. Think before you speak. But he didn't. He couldn't let Betsy think of Tripp as a viable candidate for her affections. In the long run Tripp would only hurt her and he couldn't let that happen.

"Tripp may seem nice," Ryan said. "But he's a player. Before he was married, he dated a lot of women."

Betsy cocked her head. "Other than the married part we could be talking about you."

Ryan paused. "It's different."

"Is it because you don't think he could be seriously interested in me?"

Though he wanted nothing more than to say yes, to tell her Tripp wasn't serious, thank goodness for common sense popping up a red flag. Even without a warning, there was a vulnerability in her eyes that made him want to wrap his arms around her and never let her go. A protective urge that told him he would walk over hot coals rather than say something that would hurt her. Plus, he feared Tripp *was* serious. That's what worried him.

"I don't have any doubts. You're a beautiful, desirable woman. The only thing I don't understand is why some guy didn't snap you up a long time ago."

The tenseness on her face eased and a warmth filled her blue bedroom eyes. Her lips curved up in a smile. "Perhaps that's because I was waiting for the right one."

She hadn't said that man was him but she didn't have to, because she was the woman he'd been waiting for, the one he was meant to be with forever. All he needed was the time—and opportunity--to make her fall in love with him.

Ryan was discussing a legal precedent with Lexi's husband, Nick, when Kate appeared.

She smiled at Nick. "Mind if I steal Ryan for a few minutes?"

"Of course not," Nick said easily, taking a sip of wine. "I was just about to search for my wife anyway."

The second the attorney stepped away, Kate wasted no time. She slipped her arm through Ryan's and pulled him to a private area by the fireplace.

"Why, Kate darlin'," Ryan said with a teasing grin. "I didn't know you cared."

"I do care." The smile left her lips, her expression serious. "About you. And about Betsy."

"Betsy." Alarm raced up Ryan's spine. It skyrocketed when he glanced around the room and didn't see her. "Is she okay?"

"She's fine." Kate rested a hand on his arm. "I just need to know what your intentions are toward her."

Ryan had a whole repertoire of pithy one-liners on the tip of his tongue. Then he saw the look on Kate's face and realized this was serious. "Why do you ask?"

"Betsy and I talked. I think she's confused. I just want to make sure you're as serious about her as I think you are."

"I love Betsy," he said.

Kate exhaled the breath she must have been holding. "That's what I thought."

Last year Ryan had dated the woman at his side. Now they were what they'd been meant to be…good friends. "I understand about Joel. For the longest time, I didn't."

A tiny smile lifted the corners of Kate's lips. "I know you didn't."

"When it came out that you were Chloe's birth mom, I found myself thinking it was awfully convenient that you'd fallen in love with her adoptive father."

"Joel initially thought it was a little convenient, too," Kate said with a sigh. "He accused me of using my relationship with him to get to Chloe."

"He finally realized that wasn't true." Ryan liked the happy ending Kate had found. It made him think that same happiness was possible in his life, too.

"Yes, he did."

"Betsy isn't going to believe I love her." Ryan turned and planted his hands on the window sill. He gazed unseeing into the darkness.

Kate placed a hand on his shoulder. "Why wouldn't she believe you?"

"I'm the kid who called wolf." He whirled, frustration surging through his veins. The knowledge that he had only himself to blame, fueling the anger.

"I told her I was attracted to her best friend. Now's she going to believe that I love her?" Ryan gave a humorless laugh. He'd been such a fool.

"That's how it was for me with Joel." Kate's eyes were filled with kindness rather than censure. He realized again how lucky he was to have her as a friend. "Anything I'd felt ever before paled in comparison."

Ryan shook his head in wonder. "All I want is her to know my feelings are real and aren't going to change. I don't want her to have any doubts."

"Words alone won't do it. She's going to be scared that you'll change your mind."

"I can't imagine life without her, Kate. I like hanging out with her. I like working with her on cases. We have fun together. She gets me. You know what a challenge that is."

Kate's chuckle lightened the mood.

"She's the only one I want. The only one I'll ever want." He thought of the Love Token Betsy showed him. *You and No Other.* That pretty much summed up his feelings.

"You're going to have to be patient, Ry. Show her by your words *and* your actions how much you care." Kate's eyes met his. "In time she'll come to realize you're sincere."

"She has to, Kate," Ryan said. "I don't know what I'd do if I lost her."

CHAPTER THIRTEEN

Betsy hid behind a large boulder in Joel and Kate's backyard, snowball in hand. For a while she thought that the promise of a snowball fight had been forgotten. Then after lunch the kids were sent outside to make a snow fort and to mark off the "camp" of the attacking army.

Once that was done, Kate took the two different flags her daughter had attached to broom handles and everyone counted off. Through the luck of the draw, or perhaps the unluck, she and Tripp were on the attacking team while Ryan was a defender of the fort.

"Cover me," Tripp whispered from next to her.

He had their patrol's flag in hand and this was their last chance to breech the fort and thus win the game. All of their other comrades had gotten hit and were now out of the game. The other side had lost many soldiers too. As far as Betsy knew Ryan was still playing.

"I've got five or six snowballs made up," she said to Tripp. "I'm not sure I'll be able to throw them fast enough to protect you."

"No guts, no glory." Tripp shot her a devilish smile. "If I go down, grab the flag and make a run for it."

Betsy smiled. "Deal."

"On the count of three," Tripp said, his voice filled with determination. Betsy wondered what the hospital board would think now if they could see their new administrator with his eyes blazing and snowball in hand? "One, two, thre—"

Betsy rose and began flinging snowballs.

She got Joel in the shoulder, Mary Karen in the belly. Her oldest boy, Connor, came out from nowhere with snowball in hand.

He howled with frustration when her snowball caught him in the leg.

Tripp was almost at the fort, all of his snowballs gone, flag in hand when Ryan stepped out. He stood there, with no protection, waiting for a sure shot at Tripp.

Betsy stumbled forward, one last snowball in hand. She didn't know if Ryan discounted her or if he was too focused on Tripp to give her a second thought. But she released her ball just as he raised his arm, giving her a perfect shot to the abdomen.

He looked up in surprise as Tripp planted the flag, signaling the game was over and the blue team had won.

She didn't have a chance to say anything to Ryan who was looking at her with disbelief in his eyes, because her team mobbed her, jumping up and down in the snow, chanting her name.

Betsy couldn't remember ever having quite as wonderful a day.

By the time they went inside and warmed up, the sun had already set. Tripp left, but not before giving Betsy a congratulatory hug and promising to call her.

Ryan seemed strangely silent. Of course, it could be only her imagination. She hoped he wasn't disappointed in her. After all, she couldn't throw the game just because she didn't want to hit him with the snowball.

It wasn't until they were in his truck that they had the opportunity to talk privately. "About the snowball—"

He raised one hand then turned on the highway leading back into Jackson. "I have something to say first."

"I'm proud of you, Bets."

Betsy blinked. "For what?"

"For being such a competitor."

Had he forgotten her team had won? "If I hadn't hit you with that snowball, the red team would have won. You'd have been the hero, not—"

Betsy stopped herself. To say more would feel like bragging.

"--you." Ryan smiled and took her hand, bringing it to his lips for a kiss. "That's why I'm so proud. You gave maximum effort. You didn't let anything stop you."

"You don't mind that I took you out?"

"I wish I'd played smarter and God knows I hate to lose, but it wouldn't have meant anything if I knew you'd handed me the win."

A warmth ran through Betsy's veins and she was reminded again just why she'd fallen in love with this guy.

"But the Tripp thing," he said, keeping his eyes firmly focused on the road. "I have to admit that bothers me."

"You mean that he planted the flag in your fort?"

"Forget the fort." Ryan's hand cut a dismissive swath through the air. "That was a game. I'm talking real life. I'm talking about you wanting to date him and me at the same time."

I don't want to date him, Betsy yearned to say, *I only want you.* But she kept her mouth shut.

He slanted a sideways glance. "You can date him if you want but I'm not going to date anyone else. I don't want anyone else."

Betsy slipped her arm through his and moved as close to him as the seatbelt would allow, resting her head on his shoulder. She heaved a contented sigh. "I like being with you."

Ryan's body relaxed. He took one hand off the wheel then

slipped it around her shoulder. "When we get to your house, invite me in?"

"You can come in." Betsy lifted her head slightly. "Though I don't know what I have to offer you. The fridge is pretty bare."

He pulled up to a stop light then glanced her way, his gaze dark with desire.

A fire ignited in Betsy's belly. The air became charged with electricity. Desire flowed through her veins like hot lava. She wasn't sure how she managed to keep from self-combusting before they reached her apartment. She looked for Mr. Marchand's car when they pulled into the parking lot, then remembered that he was spending the day—and hopefully the night—with his sister in Idaho Falls.

The only other obstacle to a romantic evening was Puffy. The dog ran to greet her when she opened the door then turned and bared her teeth to Ryan.

"Hey, Puffball," he said.

The dog began to bark.

"I don't know what to do with her," Betsy said, feeling the mood slip away with each yip.

"I have an idea." Ryan reached into his pocket and pulled out a bully stick. "I picked this up for her. My parents' dog used to love these."

"Puffy can be somewhat picky..."

Ryan leaned down, the stick dangling from his fingers. The Pomeranian paused mid-yap, swiveled her head and snatched it from his hand.

Betsy smiled as the animal ran across the room to sit on the rag rug in front of the sofa with her new acquisition. "I think she likes it."

"I like you." He kissed Betsy's nose.

"Want a tour of the house?"

He cocked his head, his gaze puzzled. "I think I've been in every room."

"What about the bedroom?"

The light of understanding flashed in his eyes. "I'd like to check that room out again."

Betsy reached over and cranked up the thermostat as they walked by. Once they reached her bedroom, Betsy's courage began to falter. She'd never been good at this kind of stuff...

He must have sensed her distress because he moved to her side. "I know you're probably ready to start flinging off clothes, but I'd like to just talk for a while."

She narrowed her gaze. "Are you teasing me?"

He took her hand and tugged her to the bed. When she sat down, he took the place beside her, his fingers still laced with hers. "How about we kick off our shoes and see who can make them go the farthest?"

"They'll hit the wall."

"We could see whose shoes can hit the wall at the highest point."

"Are you crazy? I don't want marks on my—" She chuckled. "Okay, we'll take off our shoes but we're not kicking them anywhere. Understand?"

Ryan slipped off one boot and then the other. "I guess I'll have to think of another game to play."

Betsy unlaced her shoes, trying to figure out what Ryan had up his sleeve.

"Is that a music box?" He pointed to a trinket box with a blue base covered with brightly colored horses in vivid colors.

Betsy leaned forward and grabbed the box. When she opened the top the horses began to revolve while the "Carousel Waltz" played. "My mother gave me this on my seventh birthday. I think it was because she knew I loved carousels."

"A thoughtful gift."

"Yes, it was." Though in recent years it seemed she could only recall the bad times, there had been some good too.

"I've got an idea for a game," Ryan said. "Have you ever played 'pass the parcel?'"

"Is that sort of like hot potato where you pass something around and when the music stops you have it in your hand, you're out?"

"Yes, except we would pass the music box back and forth and when the music stops whoever has it will take off an item of clothing and share something about themselves."

"Are you serious?"

"What's the matter? No spirit of adventure?"

Betsy thought for a second. She'd been lucky today. If her luck continued just a little while longer, Ryan would soon be naked and so would she. It was a heady thought. "I'm game."

For the first few minutes, the clothing came off slowly. A sock here. A sock there. She learned that Ryan hated asparagus but loved tuna. She shared her fear of spiders and love of anything chocolate. Now, they'd reached the point where a shirt or pants would have to come off.

The music box moved carefully between them, the sound of the tinny waltz filling the air. Ryan had just passed it to her when the sound stopped.

"Share then strip." A devilish gleam shone in his eyes. "This time something about family."

Betsy already knew her sweater was coming off. What Ryan didn't know was she had the silky long underwear beneath the sweater. Sharing something about her family wasn't that easy. She'd spent a lifetime not talking about her mother.

"How about your favorite family trip?"

Betsy started to say they'd never gone on any trips until she remembered that summer between fourth and fifth grade. "When I was ten we drove to Devil's Tower. It wasn't much to see but we sang songs and played games as we drove. Mom stopped at this old gas station and we all had bottles of orange Nehi soda pop. Keenan and I thought she might buy a beer, but she didn't."

The memory was disturbing. Had her mother quit drinking that summer and she hadn't noticed? Of course, even if she had, she hadn't stayed sober.

"Sounds like a fun trip." Ryan's eyes glittered in the dim light. "Now the piece of clothing."

"I'll take off my sweater."

"Good choice."

Betsy took her time peeling the garment over her head in a slow strip tease. When Ryan's smile faded Betsy knew he'd seen the silky long underwear.

"No wonder you weren't cold when we were throwing snow-balls," he grumbled. "You're dressed for twenty below."

She lost the next two rounds and found herself sitting before a fully clothed Ryan in only her bra and panties.

"I really like this game." His gaze remained focused on her chest.

Beneath the heat of his gaze, her breasts began to strain against the lace fabric holding them in. "I'm feeling decidedly underdressed."

"I'd like to keep it that way."

He lost the next round and took off his sweater, leaving him with a short-sleeved t-shirt.

Betsy knew she would win the upcoming round. While he'd been busy ogling her, she'd been memorizing the tune so she would know just when to hand it off to him.

He placed it in her hands and she counted the beats slowly in her head. She was ready to move it to his hand when he gasped.

"Is that a spider on the dresser?"

Betsy whirled, music box in her hands. She barely noticed that the tune had quit. Her gaze frantically searched the top of the dresser. "Where?"

"I was mistaken," Ryan said with an expression that was way too innocent. "Must have had something in my eye."

She realized suddenly what he'd done. "You, you cad. You did that deliberately."

"Did what?"

"You knew I was about to give you the music box and you deliberately distracted me."

"Betsy, Betsy, you're so suspicious." But the flash of a dimple in his left cheek told the story. "Before you take something off, tell me how many lovers you've had."

"What?"

"We both know that after you strip this time, there's not going to be much talking going on." He gentled his tone. "I want to be prepared."

"Two," Betsy mumbled. "Just two."

"When?"

"One my first year in college." She'd been so lonely then. "The other was back in Kansas City. He was another paralegal in the same firm."

"It's been awhile."

Betsy felt her face grow hot. "There's nothing wrong with that."

"No, there's nothing wrong with that," he said. "It's been a while for me too."

"You and Kate…"

"Kate and I were never lovers."

She thought of the blonde ski bunnies at the bar. "What about the girls, the blondes at Wally's Place?"

"You think I slept with them?"

"You flirt with them."

"You flirt with Tripp. But you didn't sleep with him."

"No," she said. "That would have been wrong."

He waited.

"Because," she said. "I don't care about him enough."

"But you'll sleep with me."

"Yes."

A warmth coursed through Ryan that had nothing to do with the fire burning in his belly. Betsy might say she wanted to date Tripp, but it was him that she liked, him that she trusted with her body and her heart. That's when Ryan knew everything was going to be okay.

He would win her over, show her that his love was sincere. Starting now.

CHAPTER FOURTEEN

Ryan stared at her for a long moment. The second his eyes met hers, something inside Betsy seemed to lock into place and she couldn't look away.

Then his lips curved upward in a smile that pierced her skin and traveled straight to her soul. She stood absolutely still as he reached out and touched her cheek, one finger trailing slowly along her skin until it reached the line of her jaw.

She stopped breathing when he leaned closer, brushing his lips across hers. The friction sending shivers and tingles spiraling though her body.

Betsy finally found her voice. She spoke his name, then paused, not sure what she wanted to say.

"Let me make love to you."

His request, spoken in a husky voice, sent blood flowing like warm honey through her veins. He moved his arm so her hand slid down to his and he gently locked their fingers together.

Betsy's heart fluttered. A thousand butterflies lodged in her throat. Her body quivered with anticipation. It had been a long time, but she felt sure that with Ryan it would be different. Better. Magical even.

She gazed into his eyes. Could he hear her heart pounding?

"Please," she said, not sure what she was asking for but knowing she wanted it all. Ryan was a smart guy. She was confident he'd figure out a way to meet her unspoken desires.

Before she could blink his clothes landed in a heap somewhere behind him. Like a game of follow-the-leader, Betsy took a deep breath and tossed what remained of hers on the floor next to his.

When she'd been a child, teachers had told Betsy it was impolite to stare. But she was no longer a child and she couldn't help herself. Broad shoulders. Flat abdomen. Muscular legs. And, she swallowed past the sudden dryness in her throat, indisputable evidence of his desire for her.

Heat flooded her face yet she didn't look away.

"Do I meet with your approval?" Though a slight smile teased the corners of his lips, his eyes were dark and serious.

"You'll do," she said, then belied the lighthearted tone by blushing. "What about me?"

The second the question left her lips, Betsy wished she could pull it back. There was no way she could measure up to the previous women in his life unless she dropped ten pounds, worked out for a month straight and gained a cup size.

Instead of a quick comeback, his gaze lingered. Then his eyes lifted to meet hers. "You're beautiful."

Hating that she'd put him in the position to feel obligated to offer up a sentiment he didn't feel, she ducked her head and shrugged.

"Hey." He moved closer and lifted her chin with his fingers, his eyes like molten steel. "I mean it."

Betsy shook her head slowly from side to side.

"If you won't take my word, I guess I'm going to have to show you." His voice was heavy with resignation but the gleam in his eyes told her showing was going to be a good thing.

For both of them.

Ryan took her hand and urged her to lie on the bed, then slid in beside her. Betsy's mind barely had time to register they were naked on her bed—ohmigod--when he pulled her close. He smelled of soap and a familiar male scent that made something tighten low in her abdomen.

"You are *incredibly* beautiful." His breath was warm as he spoke softly into her ear right before he took the lobe between his teeth and nibbled. "And you're all mine."

Shivers of desire rippled across her skin as anticipation coursed up her spine.

"That vanilla scent of yours drives me wild." He planted kisses down her neck while his hand lightly stroked her belly. "I want to be inside of you. I want to fill you completely until your pleasure makes you scream."

Scream? Betsy had never screamed in her life. Unless she counted the time Keenan dropped a spider down the front of her dress. Still, she was open to the possibility.

She closed her eyes and reveled in the feel of his hands on her skin. Each sensuous stroke fueled the fire building inside her. When his hand slid upward from her stomach, Betsy forgot how to breathe.

"I think," he said in a low, husky tone, "your breast will fit perfectly in my palm."

Betsy opened her eyes just in time to see Ryan's hand cup her breast. He didn't stop there. He circled the peak with his finger. Her blood began to boil. He touched the tip of his tongue to the tip of her left breast. Her need became a stark carnal hunger she hadn't known she was capable of feeling.

Thankfully he didn't stop there. Or she'd have had to beg. He circled the nipple then drew it fully into his mouth. Shock waves coursed through her body.

The gentle sucking soon had her arching against him. He couldn't seem to get enough of breasts, kissing and licking each pink peak thoroughly, dragging his teeth across the sensitive skin. She couldn't get enough of his touch.

Betsy squirmed in frustration. She pushed her hips against him, rubbing his erection. She wanted... She needed...

Even if she wasn't sure exactly what she needed, Ryan knew. His hand dipped south, slipping through her curls and between her legs.

Her breath caught in her throat as he rubbed against her slick center. No man had ever touched her like this. No man had ever made her ache like this. When his fingers found her sweet spot, she nearly rose off the bed.

"Don't stop," she begged.

"Not on your life." He kissed her and slipped two fingers inside.

Her muscles automatically tightened around them. Betsy inhaled sharply.

Ryan's lips lifted in satisfaction. "You're wet."

Was there any doubt? Betsy wanted to ask. She opened her legs wider, moving sensuously against his hand, letting him know in every way possible that she wanted more of this, more of him.

With grey eyes so dark they almost looked black, he shifted so that he knelt between her legs and began kissing his way down her belly. Part of her suspected what he was going to do while the rest of her couldn't believe it was really happening. She'd heard talk...she'd read about it in books...but no other guy had ever...

Leaning forward, he pressed his open mouth against the sensitive skin of her inner thigh. The sight of his dark head between her legs, the brush of his tongue dampening her flesh, was the most erotic experience of her life.

She rocked her hips, brazenly struggling to get the friction she needed to feed the incredible need building inside her. Her breathing came in fast pants. As the rising tension gripped her and wouldn't let go, she dug her heels into the mattress and clutched the sheets with her hands.

While fighting to catch her breath it happened. One moment she was tossing her head from side to side, every nerve ending on fire. The next she was coming apart in his arms, exploding in an orgasm that dragged a scream from her that she didn't recognize as her own.

Her body shook and she gave into the waves of pleasure coursing through her body. Once she could breathe again, Betsy opened her eyes to a world that looked different than the one she'd left moments before. It was as if she'd spent her life in darkness and someone had thrown a light switch, bathing her world in a golden glow.

A silly grin lifted her lips. "That was--"

"Unbelievably good." He kissed her lips, gently brushing her hair back from her face.

"I've never felt anything like that," she stammered, feeling like a neophyte who'd gotten her first glimpse of the Promised Land.

"That was only the beginning. There's so much more." His eyes seemed to glitter in the dim light. "Make love with me."

Betsy thought that's what they'd been doing. Apparently what she'd experienced had been simply a fantastically fabulous appetizer, a prequel to the main course which Ryan appeared eager to serve up.

"Bring it on, cowboy," Betsy said then ruined the effect by blushing.

Ryan chuckled but Betsy didn't feel like laughing when he began kissing her, branding her as his with hot moist imprints upon her skin. Sweet tension mixed with raw need.

Suddenly ravenous, Betsy couldn't wait any longer. She reached between them and guided him inside her. He was large and hard and stretched her in the best way possible. She wrapped her legs around his hips, urging him deeper.

"More," she breathed as he withdrew only to fill her again in a rhythm as old as time.

I love you. I love you. I love you. The sentiment ran over and over in her head with each thrust until she could no longer think.

"I- I—" she breathed as her body stiffened before convulsing into release a second time.

He thrust again and again until the shudders faded. She felt him plunge deep, calling out her name before burying his face against her neck.

Still intimately joined, Betsy clung to him as a languid drowsiness stole over her and his choppy breathing slowed. She knew she was grinning but she couldn't get her lips to do anything else.

Ryan kissed her hair, her lips, her neck, a matching smile on his mouth. Even when he rolled off her, he pulled her close. In between kisses and sweet caresses, they talked about anything and everything and nothing at all. Each time she thought about getting up, he kissed her again.

"I'd never—" Betsy lifted her head from his chest. Perhaps this wasn't proper post-lovemaking protocol but she really had to know. "I never experienced anything like this before. Were those other two guys total duds? Or was it me?"

Ryan almost told her it was love that made the difference. He stopped himself just in time. Because, while he knew he loved her, he wasn't sure those feelings were reciprocated. "It's the caring and the trust that made it special."

"Whatever the reason, I liked it." Betsy's well-kissed lips turned up in a satisfied smile. "I want to do it again. Now."

Her boldness delighted Ryan. "Can you at least give me a few more minutes to recover? You took me on a wild ride, cowgirl."

Betsy's hand stole under the sheets and closed around him. She grinned. "Feels to me like you're fully recovered."

Her smile faded. "Unless you don't want—"

"I want you," he said, the words a solemn vow. He wanted her not just in his bed, but in his life. He'd never wanted anyone more.

"Ah, yes." She cocked her head. "The question is for how long?"

Her tone was teasing but the look in her eyes troubled him.

"Forever," Ryan said. "That's how long."

Betsy stared at him then pulled him on top of her, kicking aside the sheet. "Let's start with tonight."

"That will do," he said. "For now."

Seconds after Ryan's truck pulled out of her driveway the next morning, Betsy was on the phone with Adrianna. "We have to talk. Can you meet for lunch?"

"I wish I could." Regret filled Adrianna's voice. "My day is jam-packed. I'm just going to grab a yogurt and eat at my desk."

"How about if I bring lunch to you?" Betsy was not going to take no for an answer. "We could eat in your office."

"Sure," Adrianna said. "I only have a half hour to spare."

After confirming the best time to stop over, Betsy hung up. Since Ryan would be in court until at least noon, he'd given her the morning off. She had to speak with Adrianna before she saw him again.

Ryan hadn't wanted to leave this morning. The way he kept kissing her and untying the chenille belt on her robe told her that much. As much as she wanted him to stay, he'd turned her world upside down. She needed time and distance to get her thoughts together and gain some perspective.

Betsy dressed in leggings and a tunic top before looking in the mirror. A new woman stared back at her. Her eyes looked darker and more mysterious. If she didn't know better, she'd say her lips were swollen from his kisses.

The change wasn't simply on the inside. Her body felt different, as if it had been asleep for a long time and had finally awakened. In the span of twenty-four short hours her life had been forever changed. She and Ryan had forged a new path.

That meant, even if they wanted to, they'd never be able to go back to the way it was before.

~

Betsy placed the sandwiches and drinks on Adrianna's desk and waited while her friend closed the door.

"What's going on?" Adrianna settled into her leather chair and unscrewed the top of her soda. "You sounded strange on the phone this morning."

"Ryan spent the night." Betsy tried but wasn't able to keep the goofy smile from her lips.

"What?" Adrianna plopped the bottle on her desk without taking a drink.

"We went to a party at Joel and Kate's yesterday and had a fabulous time." Betsy took a sip of her cherry soda. "Then he took me home and stayed over."

Adrianna's eyes narrowed. "I thought you two were just friends."

Was that disapproval she heard in her friend's voice? Had Adrianna been secretly pining for Ryan? Betsy's heart sank. Her smile faded. "Are *you* interested in him?"

Adrianna's eyes widened. "Oh, my gosh, no."

"You told me you thought he was cute."

"I do think he's cute." Adrianna's expression gave nothing away. "That doesn't mean I want to date him or see a future with him. What about you, Bets? Do you see yourself having a future with him?"

"I'd like to." Betsy paused, wanting to be completely honest with her friend. "I love him, Anna. I know he cares about me but I'm scared. How long will those feelings last? I worry that in time he'll get tired of me."

"Did he ask...to see you again?"

Something in the way her friend asked the question told Betsy she wasn't confident of the answer she'd receive. That wasn't a good sign.

Betsy nodded. "He wants to date me. Exclusively."

"So you're a couple."

"Ah, not exactly." When Betsy recalled her conversation with Ryan at Kate's house, she felt her cheeks warm. It hadn't been her finest hour.

Adrianna leaned forward, her eyes snapping with curiosity. "This sounds interesting."

"I told Ryan that Tripp wants to date me, too."

Adrianna froze. "Why would you say that?"

"Because it's true." Betsy sighed. "And because I wanted to make sure Ryan knew that another man finds me attractive. Childish, huh?"

Adrianna bit into her sandwich and chewed for several seconds. "Are you thinking that Tripp will be your backup when Ryan dumps you?"

"*If* he dumps me," Betsy protested. "Not *when*. We don't know *for sure* he's going to get tired of me. I could be 'the one.' The woman Ryan has been waiting for his whole life."

Her voice began to tremble. Horrified by how much she'd revealed, Betsy clamped her mouth shut.

Adrianna leaned forward and took Betsy's hand. "You're right. You don't know. That's why you need to tell Tripp to take a hike. You can't date him right now. You need to put your whole heart into this relationship with Ryan. Jump in with both feet. Don't sit on the edge dipping in one toe at a time."

"I don't want to be hurt."

"If he walks away from you, you'll hurt anyway." Adrianna gazed into her eyes. "Isn't that right?"

Betsy slowly nodded.

"Give this relationship your best shot. If he does walk away, it'll be his loss. At least you won't be left forever wondering if things would have turned out differently if only you'd opened your heart fully."

What Adrianna said made sense. That didn't mean the thought of putting her suggestion into action wasn't scary as hell. "How'd you get to be so smart?"

"I've made my share of mistakes." Adrianna's eyes turned dark. "I'd hate to see you make the same ones."

It sounded so simple. Give Ryan her whole heart and hope for the best. Well, she'd already given him her body and soul in addition to her heart. That meant all that was left was to hope for the best.

CHAPTER FIFTEEN

Fully focused was how Ryan normally spent the work day. Not today. This morning, all he'd been able to think of was *Betsy*.

To make matters even more complicated, he'd run into Tripp at the Courthouse. Ryan wasn't sure why the guy was there and he hadn't asked. He was still pissed that Tripp had asked Betsy out after he'd told him to back off. Yet Betsy could have said no. When he boiled it down, that's what bothered him the most.

Ryan pressed his lips together as he strode down the cavernous halls of the Courthouse. Now that he'd found the woman he wanted to spend the rest of his life with, he refused to lose her.

"Watch where you're going," a man snarled.

Ryan had felt his briefcase bump against something but hadn't realized it had been a person. He glanced up. "Chad."

The tall attorney narrowed his gaze. "You need to keep better control of that briefcase, Harcourt."

Ryan shrugged. The case had merely smacked against the attorney's leg, he hadn't swung it against the guy's head. Though after how Chad had treated Betsy, he deserved a good wallop to the head...and then some. But Ryan had promised Betsy he wouldn't hurt the guy and he was a man of his word.

Still, Chad's unwarranted irritation said something was up. That made Ryan curious. "What brings you to the courthouse?"

"What do you think?" Chad snapped. "I had business here."

He'd hit a nerve. Good.

"I heard you hired a new paralegal," he said as they both headed for the door. "How's she working out?"

"She's not with the firm anymore." A muscle jumped in Chad's jaw. "I'm not answering any more of your questions."

Yep. He'd definitely hit a nerve. Ryan smiled.

They were outside now, in the cool crisp air. The walks had been scooped, but patches of ice remained. Chad moved with long purposeful strides down the steps as if he couldn't get away quick enough. Until his Italian loafers connected with a patch of ice. The attorney waved his hands trying to regain his balance.

Ryan's smile widened as he watched the man fall on his backside. He walked up while Chad was bent over gathering the papers he'd been holding in his hand before the fall. A better man might have stopped to help. When Ryan thought about how Chad had treated Betsy, he walked past without a second glance.

After one quick stop on the way, Ryan strode into his office at two o'clock and paused by Betsy's desk. Her eyes were glued to the computer screen. When she looked up and smiled, his heart tripped over itself.

He'd hated to leave her this morning. Last night had been a major turning point in their relationship. If Betsy needed reassurance, he'd wanted to be there to give it to her. He didn't want her having any second thoughts or worrying.

Heck, who was he kidding? He wanted the reassurance.

Wanted to know that he'd satisfied her. Wanted her to tell him that she loved him as much as he loved her.

She cocked her head. "What's in your hand?"

He lifted his right arm and stared at the colors of yellow, red, white and orange in a mass of greenery as if seeing them for the first time. "I believe they're Peruvian lilies."

"They're gorgeous." Betsy breathed the words, her gaze never wavering from the bouquet.

"They reminded me of you." He handed the flowers to her. "Only not near as lovely."

A familiar rosy glow crept up her neck. "You bought them for me? Really?"

He smiled indulgently, pleased by her reaction. "You act as if a man has never bought you flowers before."

She buried her face in the bouquet and inhaled deeply, before answering. "These are my first."

Men were fools. He'd been a fool. Such beauty. Such intelligence. And that sweet—but-oh-so-sexy smile…

Ryan leaned close and kissed her on the cheek. "They won't be your last."

"Thank you." Without warning, she rose and her arms wrapped around his neck, the flowers gripped tightly in one fist. "I love…them."

For a second he thought she was going to say she loved *him*. Ryan tried hard not to be disappointed. A declaration would come in time. For now, her loving the flowers he'd given her was enough.

While Ryan had always believed in keeping personal relationships out of the work setting, he couldn't resist stealing one quick kiss.

She tasted like cherry soda, one of his favorite drinks. At least it was now. Her mouth opened and Ryan deepened the kiss. Desire, hot and insistent surged. He cupped her breast through her silk shirt, teasing the nipple with the side of his thumb.

Locking the office door never crossed his mind. Until the sound of clapping filled the air.

Betsy jerked back, the flowers falling from her fingers.

Ryan whirled, wanting to see who'd had the audacity to walk to his back offices without pressing the buzzer.

Chad Dunlop stood in the doorway, a smirk on his face. "I got to hand it to you, Harcourt. You succeeded where I failed."

Two long strides was all it took for Ryan to reach Chad. He grabbed the front of the attorney's coat and slammed him into the door frame. He'd already drawn back his fist, ready to wipe that smirk off Chad's face and shut his filthy mouth when Betsy grabbed his arm, pulling him back.

"Don't, Ryan," she begged. "He's not worth it."

It wasn't her entreaty that stopped him from throwing the punch, but something he saw in Chad's eyes. Something that told him there was more going on here. Something that said he'd be playing right into Chad's hands if he hit him.

"Get out." He dropped his fists. "Don't come back."

Chad just chuckled, turned on his heel and sauntered from the office without another word.

Ryan followed him to the front office and locked the door behind him. By the time Ryan returned to Betsy, she was picking up the last of the flowers from the floor.

She straightened, her face pale. "What do you think he wanted?"

"No idea." Ryan thought for a moment. "You were right. It was as if he wanted me to hit him."

Even knowing that, Ryan found himself wishing he'd smacked the guy. Just once. Okay, maybe twice. The thought of Chad trying to force himself on Betsy still made him see red.

Though he didn't say it aloud, he vowed he'd make sure Chad Dunlop got what was coming to him.

Ryan opened his arms to Betsy. "Come here."

Betsy shook her head, her jaw set in a stubborn tilt. "Not here. Not ever again."

The look in her eye told Ryan not to push the issue. "Can I get you a vase for the flowers?"

"You have one?"

"Several." He kept his tone light. "When Caroline worked for me, she got flowers all the time."

Betsy's eyes widened. "From you?"

"Of course not," he said. "From her husband."

"I'm sorry." A pained look crossed her face and the bleak look in her eyes tore at his heart. "I'm really making a mess of things."

"What are you talking about?" He moved close, rubbing his hands up and down her arms. Propriety be damned. This was the woman he loved and she was hurting. "It's me who can't keep his hands off of you."

"The way Chad looked at me." She shivered. "I felt so dirty."

"He's an ass." Ryan clenched his jaw. "If he knows what's good for him, he won't come around here again."

"What are you going to do if he does?" She asked with a laugh that sounded suspiciously like a sob.

"He won't." Chad had gotten off easy today. He'd better keep his distance. Otherwise, Ryan might be forced to give him a lesson in old-fashioned cowboy justice.

The next few weeks passed quickly. Betsy couldn't remember ever being happier. Ryan's friends had become her friends. Best of all she felt as if they'd accepted her for herself, rather than just as Ryan's girlfriend.

Tripp called and asked her out but she was always busy with Ryan. After a while he quit calling. Christmas drew closer and she began to believe the medallion's promise would be fulfilled, even if she couldn't find the blasted coin.

It had to be in her apartment somewhere. The medallion had disappeared around the time she and Ryan had made love for the first time. She hadn't seen it since. She'd even searched Puffy's bedding but all she'd gotten for that effort was a long stare from the tiny Pom.

Tonight, the coin barely crossed her mind. The only thing she could think of was how handsome Ryan looked in a tux. When he'd invited her to attend the Jackson Hole Hospital's annual Christmas party with him, she hadn't known what to say except, of course, yes.

Apparently, the legal work he did for the hospital had landed him a spot on their much-coveted invitation list. Betsy was excited not only because it would be the first "dressy" event they would attend together, but because so many of their friends would be there.

She waited in the foyer of the Spring Gulch Country Club while Ryan checked their coats. Though it was near freezing outside, Betsy had left her Eskimo parka at home. Adrianna had come through with a black velvet cape that was both warm and stylish.

The wrap was a perfect accompaniment to Betsy's new cocktail dress. Made of black satin, it clung to her curves in the most flattering way. She'd taken extra time with her hair and make-up and was confident she looked her best. Though Ryan had always been effusive in his compliments, if the look in his eyes was any indication, once they got home tonight, the dress wouldn't be on for long.

That was fine with Betsy, because when she'd seen him in his tux, unbuttoning the front of the pristine white shirt had been at the forefront of her mind.

After all these weeks she couldn't believe how well they meshed. Both in and out of bed. They enjoyed the same activities. Skiing. Riding bulls. Long walks under the stars when the air was so cold that Puffy had to wear a coat. Yet, on nights when the snow fell heavily and the north wind howled, merely sitting by the fire watching a movie and holding hands was fun.

"Have I told you how beautiful you look this evening?"

Her handsome Prince had returned.

Betsy turned. "About a thousand times. I wouldn't mind hearing it again."

"You are, without a doubt, the loveliest woman in the room tonight."

The sentiment was so over-the-top that Betsy had to smile. When she was with Ryan she felt beautiful.

He leaned close and lowered his voice. "After we go home, I'll *show* you just what I think of that beautiful bod of yours."

A delightful sense of anticipation skittered up her spine. Betsy placed her lips so close to his ear it was all she could do not to nibble. "Show me yours and I'll show you mine."

"C'mon you two, move it along."

Betsy straightened, immediately recognizing the deep voice with a hint of an east coast accent. "Tripp."

"Doesn't someone look extra pretty this evening." Tripp's appreciative gaze lingered.

"Thank you," she said, cursing the blasted heat rising up her neck. She wasn't sure if it was his compliment or the fact that she'd blown him off that was making her blush.

Tripp gestured with his head toward Ryan. "This guy treating you right?"

Ryan's grey eyes flashed, a warning Tripp seemed determined to ignore.

Betsy looped her arm through Ryan's. "Extremely well."

The tension on Ryan's face eased.

"Well, if he doesn't," Tripp said, obviously joking but managing to sound completely serious. "You've got my number."

"Thank you, Tripp," Betsy said.

"She won't need it," Ryan said pointedly.

Tripp just winked at Betsy, slapped Ryan on the back and sauntered off.

"I don't know where he gets off—"

Betsy placed a finger over Ryan's lips. "He doesn't matter. I'm right where I want to be."

They stood at the entrance to the ballroom which had been turned into a winter wonderland. Even the chandelier made out of antlers had white lights and greenery. Round linen-clad tables surrounded a large mahogany dance floor. Lights from flickering candles scattered throughout the room cast a romantic, golden glow.

A live band playing dance music brought men in tuxedos and women in fancy dresses to the floor. It was a world Betsy had never been exposed to but surprisingly it didn't feel at all foreign. Probably because so many of the couples in attendance were friends.

Ryan held out his hand. "Dance with me."

"How can I refuse?" Betsy gazed up at him through lowered lashes. "I've been looking for an excuse to put my arms around you since you picked me up."

Ryan led her to the edge of the mahogany floor, immediately pulling her to him. "Great minds obviously think alike."

Betsy wasn't sure how many songs they danced to, but it wasn't enough. Though her dancing skills were minimal she did fine simply following his lead. On the slower, more romantic songs, she rested her head against his chest and listened to his heart beat.

He'd told her, after one of their many lovemaking sessions that his heart beat only for her. Those words could have come from her mouth. Even though she'd been convinced that she'd loved him for years, the past few weeks had made her realize that what she'd felt before had been simple infatuation.

It was different now. She'd spent time with him and had gotten to know the man he'd become. It was that man—not the boy of her youth—who she loved. A man she would always love.

You and No Other, she murmured against his shirt front.

"What did you say?" Ryan leaned down and nuzzled her hair.

Betsy looked up, her mouth going dry at the passion in his eyes. "I, ah, the medallion is still missing."

"The Love Token?"

She nodded.

"It will show up."

"I've looked everywhere. I even checked Puffy's bedding."

Ryan's lips curved upward in an indulgent smile. "I'm betting the Puffball didn't appreciate you messing with her stuff."

Though Ryan acted as if he couldn't be bothered with the tiny scrap of a dog, she'd caught him feeding the Pomeranian bits of table food when she wasn't looking. Lately, Puffy had become his little shadow. He always acted put out but Betsy could see a bond being forged between them.

Yes, Betsy decided, life was indeed good. She expelled a happy breath.

The announcement over the PA system that dinner was about to be served caused Betsy to reluctantly lift her head from Ryan's chest. "I suppose we better find a table."

He shot her a wink. "Only if we want to eat."

"Betsy. Ryan," Cole called out, motioning them toward a table near the raised dais.

"We saved a place for you." His wife Meg smiled a warm welcome. Her gold dress was a perfect foil for her ivory complexion and auburn hair.

As Ryan pulled out her chair, Betsy returned greetings from the other couples at the table; Mary Karen and Travis Fisher, David and July Wahl and Kate and Joel Dennes.

While they ate, conversation bounced around the table, comfortable and familiar. Even when Betsy spilt cocktail sauce on her dress, she felt more chagrined than embarrassed.

She pushed back her chair. "I'm going to run to the restroom to see if I can get this out."

"I'll go with you." Kate put down her fork and started to rise.

Betsy waved her back down. "Finish eating. I'll be back in a jiffy."

The restroom was deserted, except for the attendant who gave Betsy a washcloth when she pointed to the stain, and two women refreshing their make-up in front of a long row of ornate beveled mirrors. Betsy didn't recognize either of them.

While she worked on the spot, Betsy tried to tune-out their private conversation, until she heard the name Chad Dunlop.

"The charges were filed today." The blonde in the sparkly blue dress didn't even bother to keep her voice low. "I feel sorry for Chad. It's obvious the woman is out to get him since he fired her."

"I can't believe such a respected attorney would rape anyone." The brunette widened her eyes and added more mascara to her already long lashes. "I don't know him well but I know his wife. They're a nice family."

"Prominent in the community."

"Who is the woman?" The brunette dropped the mascara in her bag then pulled out a tube of lip gloss. She added a swipe of clear shine to the red already on her lips.

Before answering the blonde spritzed the air with perfume then leaned into the falling mist. "Her name hasn't been released, but I have it on good authority she recently worked for him as a legal assistant."

A chill traveled up Betsy's spine.

"If she's the one I'm thinking of, she has several kids. Never married." The blonde's tone was heavy with condemnation. "He gave her a chance and this is how she repays him."

"We better get back to the party." The brunette pushed back her chair and stood. "Our dates are going to come searching for us."

The two laughed and left the room.

Betsy gave up on the stain and sank into one of the chintz-covered chairs they'd just vacated. Her hands began to tremble and her head spun. She forced herself to breathe. In and out. Deep breaths.

"Are you okay, Miss?" the grey-haired attendant stepped forward, her face lined with worry. "Shall I get someone?"

Betsy forced a smile. "I'm fine, thank you. Just a little light-headed."

Concern lingered in the woman's dark eyes. "May I get you a glass of water?"

"That would be wonderful. Thank you."

The woman bustled off and once the door closed behind her, Betsy rested her head in her hands, blinking back tears. He'd done it. Attacked another woman. Only this time Chad had succeeded in forcing himself on her.

It's my fault.

If she'd had the guts to go to the police and report his assault on her, maybe Chad would have been forced to get the help he needed. Even worse, her lack of action probably perpetuated his belief that he was invincible.

There was still time to do the right thing. She had to go to the police. Telling them what had happened to her couldn't help but add credence to his current accuser's story. But Betsy wasn't stupid. She knew the cost of such action. Chad and his family would seek to discredit her and everyone around her.

Thankfully the only family she had was Keenan. Her brother's reputation was already in the toilet.

Ryan.

A knife sliced into Betsy's chest, making breathing difficult. She recalled the puzzling satisfaction in Chad's eyes when he'd caught her in Ryan's arms. What had Chad said? Something about Ryan succeeding where he'd failed?

That would be his argument if she went to the police and told her story. He would say that she'd been after him, but he'd rebuffed her. Now she was carrying on an affair with her current employer. Betsy could see it now. Not only would her name be dragged through the mud, Ryan's reputation would suffer as well.

The grey-haired attendant returned, opening the door and pointing to Betsy. "There she is."

Ryan crossed the small room in two strides, his face tight with worry. If he was embarrassed to be in a women's restroom, it didn't show.

Betsy turned disbelieving eyes on the woman. "You went and got him?" Her voice rose then broke. "Why did you do that?"

Ryan crouched by her chair, his eyes dark with concern. "I was waiting outside the restroom for you and saw her coming with a glass of water. When I asked if she'd seen a woman matching your description, she told me you were ill."

"I felt lightheaded." She drew in a deep breath. "I should go home."

"Perhaps I should ask David to check you first. He's an ER physician—"

"No," Betsy said sharply then softened the word with a slight smile. "I'm sure it's nothing. If I feel worse tomorrow I'll see a doctor."

"I'll get the car and our coats." His gaze shifted to the attendant. "Would you mind staying with her for a few minutes? I'd appreciate it."

"Of course." The woman smiled at him while handing Betsy the glass of water. "I'll take good care of her."

"Thank you." Ryan pressed a twenty into the attendant's hand then turned back to Betsy. He met her gaze. "I'll be right back."

Still he hesitated, pausing to kiss her forehead and brush a strand of hair back from her face.

"He's a good man," the woman said when the door closed behind him.

Betsy nodded, tears welling up in her eyes. Ryan *was* a good man. The best. He didn't deserve the trouble she was about to bring into his life.

If she cared about him at all, she had to distance herself from him. And she needed to do it as soon as possible.

No, her heart cried out. *Not yet.*

End it now, the tiny voice in her head whispered. *For his sake.*

Rational thought warred with raw emotion on the drive home. By the time Ryan pulled to a stop in front of her apartment complex, Betsy was exhausted. He pressed to spend the night and take care of her, but she made him leave. She had a lot of hard thinking to do.

Once he left she burrowed under the covers with Puffy at her side, conscious of only one thing. The time had come to say good-bye to Ryan. And here she'd thought they had a fighting chance at happiness.

Foolish woman. Foolish, foolish woman.

CHAPTER SIXTEEN

Monday was D-Day. At the end of the day, Betsy would break up with Ryan and quit her job. Then she'd contact the county attorney and give her statement.

Thankfully she'd made enough money over the past six weeks to pay for the replacement furnace at her aunt's house. Once the house sold, she'd leave the area.

Although she loved Jackson Hole and her friends here, she couldn't be in the same area as Ryan. Sooner or later he'd find someone new to love and Betsy couldn't take the chance of running into him and his new girlfriend.

A sob rose to her throat but she swallowed it, refusing to let the tears fall. Taking a couple of deep breaths, she forced her mind on business, on the stack of work waiting for her.

She was so focused on her thoughts Betsy didn't notice the older couple waiting outside the office until she reached the door. They looked familiar. Quickly she made the connection. "Mr. and Mrs. Harcourt?"

"I'm sorry." Ryan's mother tilted her head, her grey eyes clearly puzzled. "Have we met?"

Though it had been ten years since Betsy had last seen her,

Sylvia Harcourt didn't look a day older. Instead of brushing her shoulders, her dark hair now hung just past her ears in a trendy bob. She was still as stylish as ever in a cashmere coat that put Betsy's parka to shame.

"I'm Betsy McGregor, Keenan's sister." She almost added 'and your son's girlfriend,' but she didn't. Not only because they probably already knew that, but because after today it would be no longer relevant.

"Oh, of course," Sylvia said a little too heartily which told Betsy she didn't remember at all. "How are you, dear?"

"I'm doing well." Betsy unlocked the door and motioned them inside. "Ryan should be here shortly."

"I didn't know you were working for our boy." Frank Harcourt had to be close to sixty. Unlike his wife he looked every bit his age. A bald head fringed with grey tended to do that to a man.

"It's a recent thing." Betsy flipped on the office lights. "About a month."

"He's lucky to have you." Sylvia unbuttoned her coat. "Good help is hard to find."

Betsy's smile froze. Ryan had talked to his parents since they'd become 'involved' but it was becoming increasingly obvious he hadn't mentioned her in any of those conversations. "Ryan didn't tell me you'd be stopping by."

"It was a last-minute kind of thing." Frank shrugged out of his overcoat to reveal a pair of crisply pressed navy pants and a striped dress shirt. "We're headed to Salt Lake for the holidays. That's where Ryan's sister and her family live. Ryan has been doing some legal work for us and--"

"Frank, I'm sure the girl doesn't want to hear our personal business," his wife chided.

A thin layer of ice slowly wrapped itself around Betsy's heart. "How about I make some coffee?"

"That would be nice, dear." Sylvia slipped off her coat and

gave it to her husband. He hung it on the antique coat tree next to his then wandered over to the photograph of Ryan receiving one of his bull-riding medals.

Betsy measured out the water for the coffee.

Frank shook his head. "I wish the boy would put the same amount of effort into finding a wife as he did riding those bulls."

"Ryan has dated a lot of women." Betsy wasn't sure why she'd jumped into the conversation with both feet. Once said, the words couldn't be taken back.

"He's like my brother," Frank said. "Just like him."

From the tone, Betsy surmised that wasn't a compliment. She added the packet of ground beans and turned on the coffee maker.

"Our son is not like your brother," Sylvia protested. She straightened the picture then stepped back, eying it as if to make sure it was level. "Jed is on his third marriage. Our son has yet to walk down the aisle one time."

"I'm not talking about marriages, Sylvia. The boy falls in and out of love so fast it makes my head spin. Just like Jed."

Betsy averted her eyes and pretended not to listen to the squabble.

"Oh, Frank, you know that's not—"

"What about that woman last year? Kate. All I can say about her is she lasted longer than most. Then it was Mary or Misty. No, Mitzi. That didn't last long at all. Then at Labor Day, it was Audrey."

"Is he still dating Audrey?" Sylvia asked Betsy.

Betsy thought about correcting her, but decided the name didn't matter. Adrianna or Audrey. She knew who Mrs. Harcourt meant.

"No," Betsy said in a voice that sounded hollow. "I don't believe he is."

"I tell you, Sylvia, the boy doesn't know what love is."

"Dad. Mom." Ryan stood in the doorway, a look of surprise on his face, a bag of scones in his hand.

Betsy knew the bag contained scones because every Monday, Ryan would pick them up on his way to the office. They'd enjoy them with their morning coffee. It had become a tradition. If you could call two weeks in a row a tradition.

"What are you doing here?" His gaze shifted from his parents to Betsy then back to them.

"What does it look like?" his mother asked. "We're visiting with your secretary while waiting for you."

Betsy flinched. There was nothing wrong with being a secretary. There was just something about the way that his mother said the word. Dismissive. As if she didn't matter.

"So you've met Bet—"

"We don't have much time for small talk, son," Frank interrupted. "Your mother and I need to go over those papers with you before we leave for Salt Lake."

"I want you to get to know—"

"Honey." His mother put a hand on his sleeve. "Your father is right. We don't have much time. I apologize for simply popping in and expecting you to drop everything. Surely you can spare us a few minutes."

"Mr. Fitzgibbons is driving in this morning from Idaho Falls to meet with you," Betsy reminded him. "He should be here any moment."

Ryan looked at Betsy. "Would you mind—?"

"I'll take care of him," Betsy said. "And cover things out here."

"Are you sure?" His gaze searched hers.

She forced a smile. "Positive."

"Thank you." He handed her the bag. "I brought scones."

Betsy placed the sack on the desk for the last time. So often it was hard to know when a tradition ended. But after today there would be no more scones and no more intimate conversation and laughter between her and Ryan.

Her heart did a slow, painful roll.

"I'll see you when we're done?" he asked.

"Of course she will." Her mother's comment spared Betsy the need of answering. "She works for you. Where else would she be?"

Where else indeed, Betsy thought as Ryan followed his parents out of the room.

The three had barely disappeared into his office when the phone rang. With the roads between Idaho Falls and Jackson snow-packed and more of the white stuff in the forecast, Mr. Fitzgibbons had decided against making the trip.

Betsy rescheduled the elderly man and wished him a Merry Christmas. Since they didn't have any other clients scheduled for the morning, she placed the bell on the counter and went to her office.

The door to Ryan's office wasn't shut completely. Betsy thought about closing it, but decided that might be even more disruptive.

"Betsy isn't my secretary, Mom," Ryan said, his voice tight with frustration. "She's my legal assistant. More importantly, she's my girlfriend."

Betsy wasn't surprised he told them. The only thing that surprised her was he hadn't told them before. Of course, considering how his father had gone on about his past relationships, he'd probably learned to keep his mouth shut.

Betsy slid her chair closer to the door just in time to hear his mother laugh.

"Oh, honey. For a second, I thought you said you were dating the girl."

"What happened to Audrey?" His father's voice boomed.

"Yes, Mother, that's what I said." Ryan's clipped tone spoke of his rising irritation. "Betsy and I are dating. And Dad, I don't know anyone named Audrey."

Betsy wheeled her chair closer to the door. She glanced through the tiny opening just in time to see Frank's brows pull together in a frown.

"Of course you know her. The one you couldn't quit talking about over Labor Day. Audrey."

"Adrianna?"

"It doesn't matter now." His father waved a dismissive hand. "If you can't even remember her name, she's obviously ancient history."

"Betsy is the only woman who matters," Ryan insisted.

"Honey, you can't be serious. She's your employee." His mother sounded bewildered at his vehemence. "You barely know the woman. Last time we were in the office, Caroline was here."

"What does that have to do with anything? I never dated Caroline."

"I simply meant that Betsy is very new in your life."

"I love her, Mom."

Betsy's breath caught in her throat. Though she'd seen it in his eyes, she'd never heard him say those three little words. Until now.

Betsy loved him, too. Enough to protect him from Chad. And the scandal.

"Give it time," Sylvia said in a gentle, if slightly patronizing tone. "Don't rush into anything."

"I don't need to give it time." Ryan's jaw jutted out. "Try to understand. All those other women taught me what I don't want. Now I know what I want. I want Betsy."

His parents exchanged a glance.

"All your mother is saying is to take it slow. Don't rush into anything."

"If it's true love, it will be there in six months." His mother reached across the desk and patted his hand. "If you move too fast and discover in another couple months what you felt for her was simply infatuation, it's not just you who will be hurt, but her as well."

Ryan's brows slammed together like two dark thunderclouds. He shoved his chair back.

"I'm sure that Betsy is a lovely young woman," his mother continued, softening her tone. "She deserves a man who honestly and truly loves her. Until you're sure of your feelings, don't make any promises."

Ryan rose abruptly and Betsy scooted from the door, her heart pounding. Seconds later his office door closed.

Betsy knew she wasn't the kind of woman they wanted for their successful son. She wasn't a doctor like Kate and Mitzi or a nurse midwife, like Adrianna. She was the daughter of an alcoholic showgirl. A legal assistant with a brother in prison.

In time Ryan would have seen that, too. He wasn't tired of her yet. Which meant he wouldn't be breaking up with her today.

She would have to do it. She would have to make him believe that this had just been a brief fling for her. That *she* was tired of him and ready to move on.

Because if Ryan stayed with her, Chad would end up dragging him through the mud and ruining his reputation. Nobody was going to hurt the man Betsy loved. She would protect him… even if it meant breaking her own heart in the process.

Riding bulls had taught Ryan that he had to trust his gut. Right now his gut was signaling that something was wrong. Very wrong.

He tried telling himself it was simply a stressful morning for both of them. But the set to Betsy's shoulders, the shuttered look to her eyes and the way she was too busy to share a scone and talk once his parents left told the story.

Worse yet, the day turned busy with clients coming in and out which meant there was no time for private conversation. He consoled himself with the knowledge that after work they could go somewhere quiet, have a nice dinner and he could make things right. Once he knew what was wrong.

There wasn't anything they couldn't work out. He'd seen his parents do it time and again over the years. An issue would come between them but they were always able to compromise, find common ground and a solution they could both live with. It would be the same with him and Betsy. If it was simply that she needed more reassurance that he cared, he would give it to her.

A knock sounded on his partially closed office door.

He lifted his head and widened his smile. Just the woman he wanted to see. "Since when do you knock?"

"I wasn't sure if you were off the phone or not."

Ryan ignored the fact that she hadn't returned his smile and motioned her inside. "With all the appointments done for the day, let's take off early and do something fun. What do you say?"

Still no smile.

She took the seat across the desk and folded her hands into her lap. "We need to talk."

Were there four more dreaded words in the English language? Unease slid its fingers up his spine, even as Ryan tried to tell himself this was no big deal. "What's on your mind?"

"This isn't working out."

He leaned forward, resting his arms on the table, trying to ignore his skyrocketing heart rate. Don't assume, he told himself. Speculations are dangerous. Always work with facts.

"Could you be a little more specific?" He managed to keep his voice even. "Exactly *what* isn't working out?"

"You and me."

His heart stopped. Honest to goodness stopped.

Ryan blinked and fought to find his voice. "Pardon?"

"Our relationship," she said. "It's not working."

"Since when?" His voice rose then cracked.

"For a while." She pressed her lips together and gazed down at her hands.

"How can that be?" Ryan remembered the time he'd fallen off his dirt bike and had the air knocked out of him. He felt the same way now. "Everything has been good."

She lifted her head and met his gaze. "I just don't want to date you anymore."

Panic raced through his veins even as he kept his expression controlled. "Tell me what's not working. What you don't like. We'll make it better. *I'll* make it better."

Compromise. They would compromise and everything would be as good as new, except she was saying it hadn't been good. Not for her.

"There's nothing you can do." She met his gaze. "Just like all those other women you dated that you got tired of and didn't want to date anymore. A person can't change the way they feel."

"I love you." The admission tumbled from his lips. This wasn't the way he wanted to tell her. No, never like this. But it was important—very important—that she knew how much she meant to him.

Something flashed in her eyes. A look he couldn't quite decipher but one that gave him hope. Hope that her leaving him wasn't a done deal.

"It doesn't matter," she said. "Since we won't be together anymore, it'd probably be best if I didn't work for you."

"Don't I get a say in this?" he asked, on the verge of begging.

"No."

"Don't you love me? Or even like me? Just a little bit."

For a second her tightly controlled features began to crumple but then the mask returned. "It's over, Ryan. There's nothing you can say or do to change my mind."

She rose then and turned toward the door.

"Why, Betsy," he called out to her. "Why?"

"It's for the best," she said without turning as she walked out of his office and out of his life.

Ryan slumped back in his chair and realized his parents had left out one very important detail in their relationship advice.

Compromise only worked when both parties wanted a relationship to succeed.

CHAPTER SEVENTEEN

Betsy kept her composure while meeting with the police and county attorney. She'd worried they might make her feel like a criminal but everyone was respectful. They mentioned more than once that she'd done the right thing by coming forth. If only the action hadn't carried with it such a high price tag...

I love you. That's what Ryan had said. Betsy had wanted to tell him she loved him, too. Only the knowledge that he would be hurt by his association with her made her keep her mouth shut.

This was her battle, not his. Down the road when Chad's attorneys tried to discredit her by bringing up her relationship with Ryan, his clients would be reassured by the fact that she no longer worked for him.

By the time Betsy reached her car in the courthouse parking lot, she could no longer hold back the tears. Once she started to cry, she couldn't stop.

Damn Adrianna for telling her to jump into a relationship with both feet and her whole heart. Look where that had gotten her--desperately in love with a man who would never be hers.

"Betsy." A sharp rap sounded on the passenger side window. "Are you okay?"

Betsy recognized Lexi's voice immediately. She hurriedly swiped at her eyes then shifted to face her friend.

"I'm fine." Betsy's smile felt stiff on her lips. "Just getting ready to head home."

Lexi tried the door handle. When it didn't open, she frowned. "Let me in. I want to talk."

Talk was the last thing Betsy wanted to do, especially with a woman who was Ryan's friend.

She's your friend, too, Betsy reminded herself.

She'd barely clicked the door unlocked when Lexi slid into the passenger seat. Though dressed in a black-and-grey plaid coat that looked warm, her friend shivered. "It's cold out there."

Pulling a tissue from her coat pocket, Betsy surreptitiously swiped at her nose. Small talk. Definitely manageable. For a second Betsy considered asking what had brought Lexi to the courthouse but realized the social worker might then ask her the same question. "I heard on the radio it's supposed to dip below zero tonight."

Lexi's lingering gaze brought a warmth to Betsy's face.

"I'm not sure if there's snow in the forecast or not," Betsy added. "They say there's a band of moisture—"

With gentle fingers, Lexi took her hand, stopping the babbling. "We can discuss the weather for a few more minutes. Or you could go ahead and tell me what's wrong now."

Her soft voice invited confidences. Yet, Betsy found herself reluctant to tell Lexi that she and Ryan were no longer a couple. Somehow, saying it aloud would make it seem so, well, final.

It is final she told herself. It had to be. Ryan had worked hard to build a respectable practice in Jackson Hole. She would not let his association with her ruin that for him.

Betsy took a deep breath and forced out the words. "Ryan and I, we're not together anymore."

"What happened?" Lexi released Betsy's hand and sat back, a

stunned look on her face. "You two seemed perfect for each other. So happy."

Betsy could take the questions. It was the concern in Lexi's eyes that made keeping her composure difficult. But she had to pull this off. Ryan's reputation in the community was at stake. "He wasn't the man for me. I feel badly but I had to call it quits. It's best for him."

The lies flowed surprisingly easy from her lips, but the speculative look in Lexi's eyes told Betsy the woman wasn't convinced.

"It's best for *him*," Lexi repeated slowly. "An odd thing to say."

Darn. Darn. Darn.

"I meant," Betsy stammered, "that it's best for both of us. Best for him that he's not with someone who doesn't love--" Her voice broke. She took a deep breath and tried again, "—who doesn't love him. Best for me not to be with someone I, I don't love."

Lexi's gaze searched Betsy's face. She must have seen something that answered her question because her amber eyes softened. "I'm sure someone has told you the story about Nick and how he lost his memory."

Betsy nodded, the tension in her shoulders easing. It appeared her time on the hot seat was over. Even if Lexi wasn't *fully* convinced, it appeared she was ready to give her the benefit of the doubt. Betsy was grateful. Very grateful. "You fell in love with a man who didn't even know his own name."

"That's right. What you probably don't know is that once we learned his true identity, we discovered he had a serious girlfriend back home." Lexi's eyes took on a faraway look. "By that time we were already deeply in love."

Lexi was right. This part she hadn't heard before. "What did you do?"

"Nick was certain it was me he loved, but at that point he could only recall bits and pieces of his former life in Texas. Nothing at all about the woman claiming to be his fiancée."

"Fiancée?" Betsy choked out the word. She couldn't imagine Nick with anyone but Lexi.

"Turned out Nick had never actually proposed, but I'm getting ahead of myself." Lexi shot Betsy a wry smile then continued. "Nick and I talked and we decided he should go to Dallas. We hoped that being back on his home turf would jog his memory. If he ended up wanting his old girlfriend, I told him I'd understand."

"But he didn't." Betsy already knew this story's ending. "He chose you."

"Yes." Lexi's lips lifted in a smile. "Happily his old girlfriend found her own true love, too."

The story was fascinating but Betsy had a feeling there was a point to the tale she'd missed.

"Is there something about what happened with you and Nick that you think relates to Ryan and me?" Betsy cleared her throat. "Because the two situations couldn't be more different."

"Nick and I encountered an issue that could have torn us apart but we faced it together. We discussed how we were going to handle it…together." There was a challenge in Lexi's eyes. "You and Ryan need to face whatever is going on in your life *together*."

"He doesn't—" Betsy began, then stopped, remembering what he'd said to her. "I don't—"

"You don't what? Love him. Rubbish. I've seen how you look at him." Lexi chuckled. "And Ryan is in love with you."

"You don't know that," Betsy said, a hint of desperation in her tone.

Betsy didn't want to talk about his love for her. All that did was remind her of how much she'd lost. If it was true, if Ryan *really* loved her, then she'd hurt him when she'd broken things off. For some reason that made her sacrifice seem almost selfish.

No. No. She'd done the right thing.

"I know I've never seen him like this with any other woman."

A chill traveled up Betsy's spine. The social worker speculating in the privacy of the car was one thing. If Lexi mentioned any of this to Ryan—

"This is not your business, Lex," Betsy said firmly. "Stay out of it."

The gorgeous brunette seemed more amused than offended by Betsy's blunt admonition.

"Sorry. I can't promise that." The words had barely left Lexi's lips when a car containing her husband and daughters drove up. The social worker opened the car door and stepped out but didn't immediately walk away. She leaned down and met Betsy's gaze head on. "I care about you. I care about Ryan. If I find out there's something I can do to help this situation, I'm going to do it."

Betsy watched Lexi join her family, a sick feeling in her stomach. If Lexi discovered her motive for breaking up with Ryan and decided to tell him, her interference could cost Ryan his career. Then all of Betsy's sacrifices would be for naught.

The sun had set by the time Betsy arrived home. She hurried to the front door of her apartment, eager to be inside. The key turned easily in the lock. Perhaps a little too easily. Normally, it might have given Betsy pause but right now all she wanted was to feed Puffy then collapse in a chair.

She headed toward the kitchen, noticing she'd left on the light. When she reached the archway to the room, Puffy ran to greet her. Betsy picked the dog up then stopped in her tracks.

"Dinner should be ready in five minutes." Ryan turned from the stove. "I hope you like Hamburger Helper. Potatoes Stroganoff is my signature dish."

Since she'd last seen him, Ryan had changed into jeans and a grey Denver Bronco's sweatshirt. His smile was bright—too bright--and Betsy noticed the lines of tension around his eyes.

Her heart twisted. The last thing she'd wanted to do was hurt him. But she had. She'd hurt both of them. "How'd you get in?"

"You gave me a key." He returned his attention to the skillet on the stove. "Remember?"

"I'm going to need that back." She held out her hand but he didn't look up. After a moment she dropped the hand back to her side.

Suddenly incredibly tired of the drama, Betsy sat down, hugging Puffy close. It wasn't long until the Pom began to squirm. The second Betsy released her hold, the dog jumped to the floor and trotted to stand by Ryan.

It only figured Puffy would abandon her in the hour of need. How many times had her mother bailed on her? Keenan? Even her grandmother. She'd died without warning. Betsy didn't know whether to laugh or cry watching the little dog cozy up to Ryan.

He patted Puffy on the head then stepped from the stove to the counter where a bottle and two wine glasses sat. With well-practiced ease he uncorked the bottle then filled each glass half full. "A full-bodied red should go nicely with the stroganoff."

Ryan held out a glass to her.

Betsy shook her head even as she glanced longingly at the wine.

"Take it." His eyes softened. "You look like you could use a glass."

"I need to feed Puffy and take her outside." Betsy sighed. "She's been cooped up in the apartment all day—"

"Already done." Ryan placed the glass before her on the table.

"You shouldn't—"

"I shouldn't what?" His even tone took on a hard edge. "Care about you and Puffy?"

He paused and gentled his tone. "Sorry, that's not possible."

"I think you should leave." Betsy tried but there was no conviction in her voice.

"I think you should lie down and rest," he said. "Since neither of those seem likely, let's have a nice meal with a glass of wine or two."

"But—"

"I'm your friend, Betsy. Give me at least some respect."

Betsy was too tired to argue, too tired to put up a stink and toss him out. The headache that had started when she'd been in the attorney's office and had grabbed hold when she'd cried in the car, now pounded just behind her left eye.

She rubbed her temples with the pads of her fingers. "I guess you can stay."

"You have a headache." The comment was made as an observation rather than as a question.

Betsy closed her eyes for a second. "Umm hmmm."

Moments later he appeared at her side with a glass of cola and two tablets of ibuprofen.

She glanced down at the pills. "With a cola?"

"When you take ibuprofen with a cola, it has a synergistic effect."

Betsy narrowed her gaze.

He smiled. "Hey, my sister used to get migraines and if she caught them early enough by taking the ibuprofen and caffeine, she didn't have to take her prescription meds."

Betsy popped the pills into her mouth and took a big drink of cola. At this point she'd give anything a try.

"Why don't you lie down?" He took the glass of cola she handed him without shifting his gaze from her face. "The food and wine will keep. Don't worry about Puffy, I'll keep her occupied."

Betsy wasn't worried about Puffy. She was concerned about Ryan being in her apartment, acting as if he belonged there. And about her still wishing he did.

Would a few minutes more really make that much difference? No, she decided, it wouldn't. She jerked to her feet and made it to her bedroom on auto-pilot. Slipping off her shoes, Betsy pulled back the covers and fell into her bed fully dressed.

When she opened her eyes, the clock on her bedside stand said an hour had passed. There were sounds of voices coming from her kitchen. That didn't surprise her as much as the fact that her headache had disappeared.

Betsy glanced down at her wrinkled clothes. She thought about leaving them on. After all, she could change into something more comfortable after she kicked Ryan, and whoever it was he was talking with, out of her apartment.

But her closet doors were open and comfy clothes beckoned. She slipped on a pair of yoga pants and a long-sleeved t-shirt advertising a Kansas City 5K Fun Run.

Even though dressing nice usually gave her some measure of confidence, right now comfort mattered more. She stuck on a pair of bunny slippers that Adrianna had once given her as a gag gift and ambled into the kitchen.

Mr. Marstand looked up and smiled. He sat at the table with Ryan, an almost empty plate of stroganoff and a glass of wine before him. Ryan must have already eaten because he'd pushed his chair back and held Puffy in his lap.

When the dog saw Betsy, Puffy jumped down and ran to greet her. Betsy leaned over and patted her soft fur, her heart warmed by the welcome.

"Ryan said you were a bit under the weather." Concern filled Mr. Marstand's eyes. "Are you feeling better?"

Betsy nodded and dropped into a chair at the table. "I'm not sure if it was the nap, or the ibuprofen/cola mix that made the difference, but my headache is gone."

"Good news." Ryan rose to his feet and squeezed her shoulder as he walked past. "We saved you some dinner. And a glass of wine."

"Ryan wanted to drink it all, but I told him since it was your place, a gentleman would save you at least one glass." The old man laughed as if he'd said something uproariously funny.

Betsy glanced at Ryan and they shared a smile before she realized that she shouldn't be sharing anything with him. Not a smile. Certainly not dinner. But how could she kick him out now? Not when he'd gone to all the trouble of making her a fine meal. Not with Mr. Marstand watching her every move.

"I am hungry," she said. "And wine sounds lovely."

In a matter of seconds, the plate of food that had been warming in the oven was on the table and a glass of wine was sitting before her.

Betsy had just taken her first bite when Mr. Marstand squinted behind his spectacles. "Your eyes look red. Have you been crying?"

Betsy started to choke on the stroganoff but quickly washed it down with a sip of wine. "The redness is from my headache."

Neither the older man nor the younger one looked convinced but neither pursued the topic further. They talked about the weather, the upcoming bowl games and Puffy's love of bully sticks. Then silence descended over the table.

Oblivious to the undercurrent of tension, Mr. Marstand broke the silence first. "I hear you finally got the furnace installed in your aunt's house."

Betsy looked up from the absolutely delicious stroganoff in surprise. "Where'd you hear that?"

"Well, actually we saw the billing statement on your counter." Ryan had the grace to look slightly abashed.

Mr. Marstand waved a hand. "It was sitting right there in plain sight."

Betsy didn't care. It wasn't as if the furnace was a big secret. "Yes, it's been installed. The city inspector has been out and removed the red tag from the house. I'm going over there tomorrow and start cleaning."

"Don't you have to work?" Mr. Marstand asked.

Betsy shook her head, hoping Ryan hadn't said anything about her quitting. Though her elderly neighbor liked to present a tough-as-nails image, if he knew she was unemployed, he'd worry.

Thankfully Ryan simply took another sip of his wine.

"What kind of cleaning will you be doing?" The old man sounded surprisingly interested.

"Aunt Agatha was something of a packrat, so I had a dumpster delivered today. I'm going to get there early tomorrow and start tossing things. Until I get all the junk out of there, it will be hard to clean."

And impossible to sell, she thought with a sigh.

At one time Betsy had envisioned her and Ryan working together to renovate the house. Though the place was a mess right now, it had potential. Since she and Ryan had become involved, each time Betsy had thought about the house, she'd pictured the two of them sitting together before the fireplace, eating breakfast in the little nook off the kitchen and making love in the large master bedroom.

Now, she'd be getting the house ready to sell. Another couple or family would be the ones building memories in the home, not her and Ryan.

"Tomorrow? Well, this is your lucky day, missy," Mr. Marstand said. "I usually go to Bingo on Tuesdays but it got cancelled. Which means I'm available. What time do you want to start? I can be ready by six. Is that too late?"

Six? Was he kidding? "Ah, I was thinking of starting around nine."

"That'll work." The older man shifted his gaze to Ryan. "What about you, son? Will that time work for you?"

Betsy tightened her hand around her wine glass. Nonono. This situation was rapidly getting out of control.

"Absolutely." Ryan kept his gaze focused on Mr. Marstand. "I'll have my truck if we need to haul any cleaning supplies, ladders, stuff like that."

"Good thinking." The older man nodded his approval before pushing back his chair and standing. "I hate to eat and run, but my favorite show will be on the tube in five minutes."

"I'll walk you out." Ryan stood. "I've got a few things I need to do yet this evening, too."

Mr. Marstand cocked his head. "Don't you want to stay and keep Betsy company while she eats?"

"I'd love to but I have an, ah, an appointment." Ryan edged toward the door.

"Ryan, honey," Betsy said in a sugary sweet tone. "Please stay. There are a couple things we need to discuss."

She needed to make it clear that while she appreciated his efforts tonight, this was not happening again. He was out of her life. It might not make sense now but one day he would thank her for it.

"Sorry, can't." His hand curved around the door knob. "My, ah, my mom is expecting me."

"In that case you have to go," Mr. Marstand said before Betsy could say a word. "A man can't keep his mother waiting. Isn't that right, Betsy?"

Betsy tried to meet Ryan's eyes, to say in a glance what she couldn't say with Mr. Marstand standing there hanging onto every word. Ryan looked everywhere but at her.

"I'll see you tomorrow." He opened the door and stepped aside to allow Mr. Marstand to pass, reaching out to steady the older man when he started to wobble.

Betsy rushed toward the door. The fact that he was out of her life had to be made clear before he got out of her sight.

"Ryan," she called out, her bunny ears flopping up and down with each step, "I want you—"

He reached out a hand and pulled her to him, his lips closing over hers. Her head told her not to respond. Her body had different ideas. By the time he broke off the kiss, she was swaying and her thoughts were a tangled mess.

Her head was still spinning when he headed down the steps. When he reached the bottom, he turned and smiled. "I want you too, sweetheart."

No, she wanted to call out, *I want you out of my life*. But she remained mute as he jumped into his truck and drove away.

She wanted him. That hadn't changed. But getting him out of her life? She touched her tingling lips. That was proving to be a far more difficult task.

CHAPTER EIGHTEEN

Ryan drove slowly through downtown Jackson, encouraged but still frightened. He'd never admit the frightened part to anyone. He'd ridden two-thousand-pound bulls and never once been afraid. Yet the thought of losing Betsy filled him with icy fear. Even though she'd kissed him like she didn't want to let him go, he had the feeling she still planned to walk away. He just wasn't sure why.

Traffic was heavy but Ryan didn't mind. Going home held little appeal as did stopping at Wally's Place. Though it was "Ladies' Night" and the bar would be crawling with women, there was only one-woman Ryan wanted and she wouldn't be there.

As he slowed his truck for a turning car, he noticed that Hill of Beans was still open. Though it didn't make sense to flood his system with caffeine this late at night, he turned into the parking lot.

Ryan pushed open the door to the coffee shop and breathed in the rich aroma. White lights and brightly colored bulbs decorated a large fir tree sitting in front of the plate glass window. Garlands of coffee filters—hand decorated by patrons—added a festive air to the exposed brick walls and beamed ceilings. It was hard to believe twenty-four hours ago, Ryan had actually been excited for Christmas.

It would have been his and Betsy's first Christmas together, the first of many to come. Now it was looking like they might not make it to *this* Christmas...

No. Ryan shoved the thought aside before it had a chance to fully form. Betsy and he would be together. Failure wasn't an option.

"Look what the cat dragged in." Cole's broad smile of welcome belied his words.

"I can't believe you're actually working, Lassiter," Ryan shot back. "I thought you'd be home counting your money."

Cole not only owned this store but was head of the Hill of Beans empire. Last Ryan knew, his childhood friend had something like fifty or sixty stores in multiple states.

"There's a big holiday show at the high school tonight." Cole ignored the jibe. "I didn't want the kids who work here to miss it, so I volunteered to fill in."

"How are Meg and Charlie?"

"Charlie's growing like a weed," Cole said with a proud papa smile. "Meg just finished her first trimester so she's starting to get her energy back."

A baby. Ryan fought a pang of envy. Before now he hadn't thought beyond the fact that he wanted kids. Now he knew he wanted Betsy to be their mother.

Cole rested both hands on the counter, relaxed and confident, with an easy smile on his lips. After a dismal childhood, Ryan was glad his friend had finally found the happiness he'd long deserved. "What's your pleasure?"

"A small coffee should do it."

"I'll pour a cup for myself and join you." Cole lifted a brow. "If you feel like company, that is."

"Sure." The last thing Ryan wanted was to be alone with his thoughts.

Once Cole sat down, they talked sports for a few minutes. They'd just moved on to the upcoming football bowl games when the bells over the door jingled.

Both men turned in their seats.

Cole pushed his chair back then lifted a hand in greeting to Nick and Lexi.

The two had been laughing about something when they'd walked through the door and their laughter carried easily into the shop.

Another happy couple, Ryan thought with a trace of bitterness.

It had once seemed as if everyone had someone special in their life but him. Then Betsy had come along and he'd realized the wait had been worth it. Now, she said she didn't want him…

"What brings you out on such a cold night?" Cole asked.

Nick grinned. "If you could see the back of our SUV, you wouldn't have to ask. Lexi closed out three stores."

His wife punched him playfully in the side. "What my darling husband is trying to say is that we've been Christmas shopping."

"And I've loved every minute." Nick looped an arm around her shoulders. "Coraline is keeping the girls overnight so we're making the most of the evening."

The successful family law attorney shot his wife a look that said the night was far from over.

Ryan took a sip of coffee, relishing the heat on his tongue. A couple of days ago that could have been him and Betsy enjoying an evening out while anticipating a night of pleasure once they returned home.

Cole moved behind the counter and smiled at the couple. "What would you like? It's on the house."

After giving their orders the two wandered over to where Ryan sat.

"May we join you?" Lexi asked.

"Absolutely." Nick pulled out a chair. "We'll be much better company than Cole."

"I heard that." Cole returned to the table with their drinks. "Just for that, a tip is mandatory."

Once they were all settled around the table, Ryan expected one of the three to ask about Betsy, but they ended up talking about some foster kids that Lexi had to place on an emergency basis that afternoon.

"I didn't leave the courthouse until after five thirty. I'm happy to report the children now have a home for the holidays," Lexi announced with a satisfied sigh.

"Did you happen to run into Chad Dunlop while you were there?" Cole asked.

Ryan stiffened at the name.

"I didn't." Lexi cast Cole a curious look. "Should I have?"

"Rumor is the county attorney is getting ready to charge Dunlop with first degree sexual assault," Cole said in a matter-of-fact tone.

Ryan straightened in his chair. "Where'd you hear that?"

Cole chuckled. "It's amazing what you learn when you stand behind that counter for an hour or two."

"I heard that same rumor earlier today," Nick admitted.

Lexi turned to her husband. "You never mentioned that to me."

"I didn't know you'd be interested." Nick shrugged. "We barely know the guy."

Ryan took a calming breath, determined to keep a conversation tone. "Either of you have details?"

"Only that a former legal assistant claims he sexually assaulted her when they were working late." Nick leaned back in his chair and shook his head. "Helluva thing."

A chill traveled through Ryan's body.

If Keenan hadn't taught Betsy how to defend herself…

If she hadn't gotten lucky and placed her knee in just the right spot…

Lexi's curious gaze settled on Ryan. "You don't seem surprised."

"I'm not." Ryan pressed his lips together, telling himself not to say anything more. He couldn't help himself. "Dunlop is an animal."

"Didn't Betsy used to work at his firm?" Lexi asked in a voice that was a little too casual.

Ryan gave a short jerky nod.

"Did she have any trouble with him?" Nick asked, his gaze narrowing.

"I saw Betsy today in the courthouse parking lot," Lexi said when Ryan didn't immediately answer. "She was upset. I wonder if her tears had something to do with Chad."

"She was crying?" Ryan clamped down on the rage building inside him.

Lexi nodded. "She mentioned you and she were having problems."

Ryan could read between the lines. She'd told Lexi they'd broken up. Which meant she was serious about her plan to push him out of her life. But why now? With all this stuff with Chad going on, you'd think she'd want him by her side for support. Unless...

The image of Chad in his office doorway, clapping, with that pleased expression on his face flashed before him. The puzzle pieces that had been floating around in Ryan's head began to lock into place. When he'd caught them together, Chad realized if Betsy ever came forward with her story, he could use her relationship with her current employer—him—to discredit them both.

Was breaking up with him a misguided attempt on Betsy's part to protect him? Surely not. Surely she realized he could protect himself. Her too, if given the chance. Still, his possible explanation made more sense than her claiming out of the blue that she didn't care about him anymore.

Protecting him had to be the reason she'd walked away.

"What's going on, Ry?" Cole asked quietly.

Ryan ignored the concern in his friends' eyes. "Nothing that I can't remedy."

"You don't have to do it alone," Cole said. "If there's anything Meg and I can do to help, just let us know."

"Same here," Nick said.

Lexi placed a hand on his arm. "You and Betsy have a lot of friends in this town. Remember that."

Ryan stood, his mind racing. "I appreciate the offers."

Tonight he'd plot a course of action.

Tomorrow he'd implement that plan.

She didn't know it yet but soon Betsy would be back where she belonged. With him. They'd stand strong and face whatever Chad threw at them...together.

The day had dawned overcast and cold but Ryan appeared in a particularly sunny mood when he stopped by Aunt Agatha's. Betsy had her speech prepared. Coming up with just the right words had kept her up most of the night.

She would make sure Ryan understood that he had to leave and not come back. Betsy glanced out the living room window and watched him load blankets and clothing into his truck bed to take to the Good Samaritan Mission on Pearl Street.

Since the wind held an icy bite, Ryan had put on a blue stocking cap to keep his ears warm. Mr. Marstand was outside too, hood up, wearing the extra coat the attorney had brought with him. Ryan had said the garment was too small and had offered it to Mr. Marstand.

The older gentleman had eagerly accepted. He was soon raving about the coat's thick lining and warm hood. That's when

Betsy realized that her neighbor had worn those light jackets, not out of choice, but out of necessity.

Shame flooded her. She'd been so focused on her own problems that she hadn't even noticed a neighbor in need.

Betsy had been prepared with her speech when Ryan had arrived, but when he'd presented the old man with the coat, she hadn't wanted to mar Mr. Marstand's obvious pleasure with ugliness.

Her new plan was to wait for the two men to come inside. Then she'd send Mr. Marstand on an errand so she and Ryan could talk privately. While waiting Betsy busied herself piling last year's newspapers into a metal shopping cart she'd found in the yard.

"My lordy, it's cold out there." Mr. Marstand pulled the front door shut against the brisk north wind, his wrinkled cheeks bright red.

If Betsy didn't know better, she'd swear the man had bits of ice clinging to his mustache. "How's the coat?"

"Best I ever owned." Mr. Marstand lowered his voice to a confidential whisper. "I don't think it's ever been worn. I'm surprised the boy didn't take it back when he realized he'd gotten the wrong size."

"You know how it is." Betsy waved a hand. "You get busy. Then all of a sudden too much time has passed for a return."

"Well, I sure do appreciate him thinking of me."

Betsy peered over his shoulder, as if expecting the attorney to open the door and magically appear. "Is Ryan still loading the truck?"

"He left."

Betsy inhaled sharply. She'd wanted Ryan to leave, but not before she spoke with him. "Where did he go?"

Mr. Marstand shrugged. "Said he had some business that needed attention."

Betsy wasn't sure if the sensation coursing through her was

relief or disappointment. Or maybe surprise that he'd left without saying good-bye. Of course, Ryan could have picked up on her coolness toward him and decided he'd had enough. A knot formed in the pit of her stomach. "Did he mention coming back?"

"Don't worry." Mr. Marstand patted her arm. "He'll be back. That boy likes being around you."

The words shouldn't have made her feel better. But they did.

Betsy changed the subject by pointing to a stack of magazines. "I have all this stuff I don't want while the one thing my aunt gave me that meant something has disappeared."

Mr. Marstand bent over and took an armful of the magazines, dropping them in the cart on top of the newspapers. "What's missing?"

"A Love Token." Betsy chewed on her lower lip, trying to decide the best way to describe it. "It looks like a coin. It has ivy and hearts and—"

"Stop right there." Mr. Marstand reached into his pocket. "Is this it?"

Betsy gave an excited shriek. "Where did you find it?"

"On the sidewalk in front of the apartment building. Didn't know who it belonged to." He flipped it to Betsy. "Do you know what the words mean?"

She slipped the medallion into the pocket of her jeans, pushing it way down so that there was no chance of losing it again. "You and No Other."

Mr. Marstand thought for a moment then smiled. "That's how your young man feels about you."

"Ryan isn't my young man." Betsy hardened her heart against the stabbing pain. "We broke up."

There she'd told Mr. Marstand. Another step forward.

"You two don't look broke up to me." Mr. Marstand picked up the last of the stack of magazines and tossed them into the cart.

"That's because he won't go away," Betsy said more crossly than she'd intended.

"He loves you."

Betsy acted as if she hadn't heard the comment. "Is that all the magazines?"

"Yup." The old man lifted a misshapen plastic toy horse from a stack of junk and handed it to Betsy. "What's the story on this fella?"

Betsy swallowed a sigh. From one topic she didn't want to discuss to another.

"My mom stepped on it when she was drunk." Betsy kept her tone matter-of-fact. "Aunt Agatha tried to glue it back together. I don't know why she kept it. I told her to throw it away."

Betsy couldn't help caressing the palomino's nose. The horse had been precious to her. A birthday present from her aunt, the year her mom had forgotten the day entirely. "Mom never even apologized. Not about the horse or forgetting my birthday."

A look of understanding mixed with sadness filled the old man's gaze. "I had a daddy who liked the bottle. Like your mama he never apologized for nothin'. Mam said it was 'cause he didn't recall doin' it."

"My mom used to say horrible things to both me and Keenan."

"That was the alcohol talking." The lines on Mr. Marstand's face appeared to deepen. "Pap used to tell me I was worthless and more trouble than I was worth. My sis used to cry when he said that to her. Not me. I never cried."

"Keenan never cried either."

"I told everyone the words just bounced off me like one of them bouncing balls." Mr. Marstand gave a humorless chuckle. "It sounded good."

"My mom's words hurt," Betsy admitted. "I tried not to let her actions—or her words—affect my life."

"Sometimes they still do, just in ways we can't see."

Even if Mr. Marstand hadn't been staring at her with that expectant look on his face, she'd have made the connection. "You think my past is affecting my relationship with Ryan."

"Isn't it?"

Though she didn't owe her neighbor an explanation, Mr. Marstand was much more than simply the man next door. He was her friend. The grandfather she'd never had.

"No, it isn't. There are reasons Ryan and I can't be together," Betsy said. "Big, important ones."

"Have you shared those big important reasons with him?"

Betsy shook her head.

"Then I think it's about time. Don't you?"

CHAPTER NINETEEN

Ryan left the Teton County Court House with most of his questions answered. At first, he'd encountered some resistance. Until he'd mentioned he was there representing Betsy's interests. Was it his fault they took that as saying he was her attorney?

After hearing the details of the case against Chad, Ryan knew why the prosecutors were so grateful Betsy had come forward. Although there was good forensic evidence, the legal assistant Chad had assaulted had a few things in her past that the defense would likely use to their advantage.

With Betsy also reporting inappropriate actions, the chance that they would get a conviction had increased exponentially.

Ryan knew that surprises were never a good thing. He mentioned to the district attorney that Betsy now worked for him and that they were involved. He didn't stop there. Ryan made it clear he expected Chad's legal team to use that fact to discredit her.

Had he coerced Betsy into that relationship? the attorney had asked. Was any intimacy consensual? When Ryan made it clear that Betsy was the woman he wanted to marry and that anything that happened between them had been consensual, the tense set to the DA's shoulders eased.

All that was left was for Ryan to go to Betsy, explain what he'd done and tell her there was no obstacle to keep them from being together.

Only one thing worried him. What if this wasn't why Betsy had broken off their relationship? What if she simply didn't love him?

What was he going to do then?

Betsy took Mr. Marstand home then returned to the house. The sun had set and the house that had been comfortable at 52 degrees while they'd been working had taken on a decided chill.

If she emptied more closets or cleaned out a few more cupboards, she might have been able to keep warm. But she was tired of working. Tired of wondering why Ryan hadn't returned.

Not that she wanted him to, but it was rude to promise to come back and then not to even call. Still, even if he did call, she wasn't really in the mood to talk. Mr. Marstand had given her a lot to think about. Who knew the quirky octogenarian was such a sage?

Pulling a musty smelling crocheted Afghan from the table, Betsy wrapped it over her coat and leaned back in the chair. In the past when a childhood memory surfaced, she pushed it back.

For the first time, Betsy let the memories wash over her. Happy ones. And not-so-happy ones.

She recalled the drunken binges, the broken promises, the horrible things said in anger. To her surprise, she remembered a few happy times too. Times when her mother's eyes had been clear and bright. Times when they'd laughed and sang songs. Times when her mother seemed genuinely glad to have a son and a daughter.

Her mother had never asked for her forgiveness. Now, because she was dead, that would never happen. What had that minister said? Something about grace being needed but not deserved?

Could she forgive her mother? Let go of the hurt? Put aside the anger?

She'd seen evidence of the rage that burned inside Keenan. Though he was innocent of the charges that had sent him to prison, he'd been a time bomb waiting to explode. It would have been only a matter of time until he'd really hurt someone or himself.

Betsy closed her eyes and summoned up an image of her mother and the trip to Devil's Tower. When they'd stopped for gas. When she'd returned to the car after paying and surprised Betsy and Keenan with the bottles of orange Nehi soda.

Another good moment, Betsy thought in surprise. Good times that she'd nearly forgotten.

"I forgive you," Betsy whispered. Then, because it seemed if you were going to forgive someone, the words should be said with more certainty, with more gusto. Betsy took a deep breath and tried again. "I forgive you, Mother," she called loudly, her words echoing in the silent house. "For everything."

At first nothing happened, other than some fluttering in the attic. Then, like a warm summer rain that washes everything clean, the hurt and anger Betsy had been holding onto since she'd been a child, let go of her heart and the tension in her chest eased.

Betsy glanced around the darkened living room. Nothing had changed on the outside. On the inside, well on the inside, the sun, which had been covered by clouds, was shining brightly.

~

Since the sidewalk leading up to her apartment was wet, Betsy carried Puffy from the car. She sniffed. "Puffball, I don't know if it's you or me, but one of us needs a bath."

Betsy figured it was probably both of them. Aunt Agatha's home had a musty, foul smell that made Betsy wrinkle her nose each time she walked through the door. Soon it would be clean. The hardwood floors would be resurfaced and waxed and lace curtains would hang at bright and shiny windows.

She pictured Ryan and Puffy bursting through the door and her opening her arms to hug them both.

Stop it, she told herself. What Mr. Marstand had said was all well and good, but she refused to let Ryan be hurt because of her.

Puffy began squirming in her arms, making pulling the house key from her pocket even more difficult. Then her phone rang.

Betsy dropped the dog to the porch and gave her the hand signal for "sit" while she pulled out the phone. "Hello."

She listened in disbelief as the district attorney told her the preliminary hearing on the charges against Chad had gotten moved up to tomorrow. Apparently, Chad didn't want the 'unpleasantness' hanging over him during the Christmas holiday. There was an opening on the docket and his attorney took it.

"I can be there," Betsy said. The phone cut out for a few seconds. She thought he said something about having her attorney there for support but he knew she didn't have an attorney. "I'll see you at ten."

After retrieving the key from her purse, Betsy opened the door and found herself face-to-face with Ryan.

Puffy, the traitor dog, jumped up and down like an acrobat on a trampoline. Betsy had to admit, her own heart had given a little leap. Just one. Okay, maybe two.

Betsy shouldered past Ryan, inhaling the clean, fresh scent of him. Not only did he smell terrific, he looked even better. Black pants. Crisp white shirt with cuffs rolled up.

"You know breaking and entering is a crime," she said, acutely aware of her own disheveled appearance.

"I have a key." He smiled. "How many times do I have to remind you?"

"Yes, well—"

"What's that smell?" Ryan sniffed then wrinkled his nose. "Is that foul odor coming from you?"

Betsy felt heat rise up her neck. "It's my aunt's house. The smell must have gotten in my clothes. Maybe even in my hair."

Before she knew what was happening, he'd unzipped her parka and slipped it off, holding it at arms' length. "I'll hang this out on the back deck to air out," he said. "While you take a shower."

Who was he to order her around her own home? Although she had to admit, the smell was a bit overpowering. "Excuse me. This is—"

"No need to thank me," he said. "I'll feed Puffy then take her outside. I don't think she smells."

He caught the dog mid-leap then sniffed while Puffy tried to kiss him. "Nope. She's fine. It's just you."

"Go on," he said when she hesitated. "You don't want your apartment to start stinking."

With a little yelp, Betsy ran off down the hall. Once she was out of earshot, Ryan dropped his gaze to the small red dog, staring up at him with a skeptical expression.

"You're right, Puffy, she didn't really smell all that bad. But when a guy asks a woman to marry him, I think she'd like to smell like vanilla, rather than musty old gym socks."

Betsy took her time in the shower, wanting to make sure no trace of that horrible odor remained on her skin or in her hair. Only when she was absolutely certain that it was all gone did she step from the shower. After slathering her skin with her favorite cherry-vanilla scented lotion, she took a few minutes to dry her hair.

She heard pots clanging in the kitchen which meant Ryan was making dinner again. Although she'd allowed it once, this time she was putting her foot down. First she was dabbing on a little make-up and pulling out the flat iron.

Betsy strode into the kitchen about ten minutes later. Though she'd been tempted to put on her feet pajamas, she decided that might send a mixed message. She settled for her favorite skinny jeans and an oversized turquoise sweater.

"You look fantastic." Ryan glanced up from a pizza crust he was decorating with her stash of olives, mushrooms and green peppers. He lifted his head and sniffed. "You smell even better."

His grin was so infectious she couldn't help but return his smile. Until she remembered he must leave and that she needed to make him.

"I want you to go."

Ryan cocked his head and looked at her with a quizzical expression. As if she'd spoken a language he didn't understand. "The pizza is almost ready to go into the oven," he said. "I saw some romaine in the fridge. Why don't you toss together a salad and I'll uncork the bottle of wine?"

"I'm not hungry." The comment might have been believable if her stomach hadn't growled.

He smiled and Betsy realized she wanted nothing more than to let him stay. She wanted to sit across the table and share her conversation with Mr. Marstand. She wanted to tell Ryan she'd forgiven her mother. She wanted to talk to him about the preliminary hearing tomorrow. Most of all, she wanted him to hold her in his strong arms and tell her everything would be okay.

But he had to leave. Or did he?

You and Ryan need to face whatever is going on in your life together, Lexi had urged.

Have you shared those big important reasons with Ryan? Mr. Marstand had asked.

After all the chaos she'd experienced growing up, Betsy prided herself on being a rational woman. One who looked at all sides of an issue and arrived at a logical conclusion.

That's what she thought she'd done with Ryan. She'd logically concluded that he—and his practice--would be badly hurt because of his involvement with her.

It didn't have anything to do with feeling she didn't deserve to be happy. She wasn't self-destructive, not the way Keenan had been. Or Mr. Marstand's sister.

She was doing this for Ryan. Walking away from the man she loved in order to protect him. The problem was he refused to let her walk away. He kept coming around. This was a complication she hadn't foreseen. It didn't make sense. He'd left or let all those other women leave him without any fuss. Why was he being so stubborn now? Betsy raised a hand to her head, as if that could stop the spinning thoughts.

"Is your headache back?"

She glanced up to find him standing beside her, his eyes filled with concern.

"You would have eventually left me anyway, right?"

He didn't act as if he didn't know what she was talking about, didn't make a joke or brush the question aside. He gazed into her eyes and said very simply. "I will never leave you."

Betsy wasn't sure how to feel about that answer. On one hand his loyalty thrilled her. On the other, it terrified her. How was she going to protect him if he wouldn't let her?

"I love you, Betsy." Ryan's voice deepened with emotion. "You're the woman I've been waiting for my whole life."

There was a part of Betsy that wanted to wrap the sweet words around her heart and hold them close. The logical Betsy knew it didn't matter what he thought he wanted. She had to protect him.

"You've liked a lot of women," she said pointedly, trying to defuse his earlier words.

"Yes, Betsy, I've liked a lot of women. *Like* being the operative word." Ryan took her hand and led her to the sofa. He brushed the Pom off the sofa, ignoring Puffy's startled look, then pulled Betsy next to him as he sat down.

"We don't need to have a big conversation about your dating history." Betsy's voice sounded breathless, even to her ears. "I was simply making small talk until I asked you to leave. I'm asking you now. To leave, I mean. This time don't come back."

The words were all there. The problem was her delivery lacked any real oomph. That was probably why Ryan merely blinked and shifted to face her rather than grabbing his coat and heading out the door.

"I'm not going anywhere." His hand slid down her arm, leaving goose bumps in its wake. "The reason you're having such difficulty making me leave is—"

"Because you're stubborn."

"No," He caressed the palm of her hand with his thumb. His stroking fingers sending shock waves of feeling through her body. "You don't really want me to go. Do you know why?"

It was difficult for her to think. How could such a simple touch be so sensual? She pulled her hand back. "No. But I'm sure you're going to tell me."

Time seemed to stretch and extend.

"Because you love me as much as I love you."

"You don't love me," she said automatically.

Ryan's expression didn't change. It was as if she hadn't even spoken. He stared at her for a long moment, his eyes boring into hers. "Do you love me?"

"What?"

"Answer the question," he said in a courtroom voice that left no wiggle-room. "Do you love me?"

"Yes," Betsy blurted out, then instantly realized her mistake. "I mean no. I don't."

"Now that we've got that settled," Ryan's mouth lifted in a slight smile, as if pleased by her response. "I'm going to tell you a story."

Somehow without her noticing, he'd moved closer. Too close. A smoldering heat flared through her. It took several erratic heartbeats for Betsy to find her voice. "Once you tell your story, will you leave?"

"When I finish, if you want me to go, I will." Despite his serious tone, there was a smile lurking in his eyes again.

"Okay." Betsy sat back and crossed her arms. "You may proceed."

The colored lights from the Christmas tree bathed Ryan's face in a golden glow. Betsy stared, mesmerized.

"Once upon a time, there was a prince. He had a wonderful family, friends he respected and a career he enjoyed. But the prince was lonely. He wanted a princess to join him in his kingdom."

"First time I ever heard anyone refer to Jackson Hole as a kingdom," Betsy muttered.

He ignored the interruption. "There were lots of beautiful princesses for this handsome prince to choose from…"

Betsy snorted.

Without warning Ryan bent his head and kissed her softly on the mouth.

"Hey, what—"

"Every time you interrupt, you get a kiss. Now, may I continue?"

Betsy nodded, resisting the urge to touch her lips.

"While there were lots of beautiful princesses, not just any princess would do. When the prince came upon Princess Betsy, he realized he'd found the one he'd been waiting for his whole life. But there was a problem."

His eyes seemed to glitter, suddenly looking more black than grey.

"Chad Dunlop." The name popped out before she could stop it.

His eyes dropped to her mouth. Leaning close, he kissed the base of her jaw, his breath warm against her neck as he spoke, "The problem was Princess Betsy didn't believe Prince Ryan loved her. She didn't trust him."

Betsy pulled her brows together. If he was telling a story, he should at least try to be factual. "I trust you."

He took the fingers of her hand and kissed them, feather light. "Not enough to tell me about Chad and the upcoming hearing."

Betsy inhaled sharply, snatching her hand back. "You know?"

He nodded.

"So you understand why we can't be together."

"No." He shook his head. "I don't understand at all."

Ryan was a smart guy. The fact that he didn't seem concerned about the hearing only added to her worry. "You saw how Chad acted in the office the other day. He'll make it look like you're a fool taken in by my charms."

"I'm not sure about the fool part." He shot her a teasing grin. "I have been taken in by your charms."

"Be serious. I won't let your association with me damage your reputation." Tears filled Betsy's eyes. "Please, Ryan. I'm not worth it."

His head jerked up.

Betsy didn't know which of them was more surprised. *Not worth it?* Did she really feel that way? Had Mr. Marstand been right? Had her past affected her more than she'd realized?

"You are worth it, Betsy. Don't worry about Chad's attorney. He might try to discredit us but it won't work." Ryan slid his fingers through her hair. "We love each other. There's no shame in that."

"Your association with me could damage your reputation," she repeated, her voice cracking.

"If that happens, we'll deal with it." His gaze searched hers. "Being with you is all that matters to me."

Her heart swelled in her chest and she hugged the sentiment close. But Ryan wasn't being rational. He needed to look at what he'd be giving up, what he stood to lose if he was wrong. Having his good name and his reputation tainted by scandal was a real possibility. Chad was crafty and the attorney he'd hired was the best in the region.

Ryan's gaze scanned her face. The moment his eyes touched hers, something inside Betsy seemed to lock into place and she couldn't look away.

"I can survive losing my career." He cupped her face in his hand. The raw emotion in his eyes took her breath away. "I can't survive losing you."

Betsy's heart rose to her throat. Forgiving her mother had been only the first step in throwing off the shackles of the past. Trusting in Ryan's love and feeling worthy of that love was the next step. Could she take that step? Was she ready?

"I love you," she murmured. Then, because something so important should be said with gusto, she said it again. Only this time louder and with all the passion in her heart. "I love you, Ryan. I don't want to live my life without you."

He let out a long breath but waited, as if sensing she wasn't finished. As if knowing there were still words welling up inside her that needed to be shared.

"From the time I was ten I was convinced I loved you. I realize now that it was mere girlish infatuation." Betsy fought the urge to drop her gaze to her hands. Instead, she focused on his eyes, those beautiful grey eyes that held so much love. "Spending time with you has made me realize how superficial those feelings were. My feelings for the man I've come to know these past six weeks are anything but superficial. They're deep and true. I'll never love anyone more than I love you."

"You and No Other." A sudden look of tenderness crossed his face. "That's what the coin says."

Betsy nodded.

"That's how I feel about you." His voice grew husky. "That's why I had those words inscribed inside the ring."

Before she knew what was happening, Ryan took her hand then dropped to one knee. He reached into his pocket and pulled out a diamond ring. The large marquis-cut stone caught and scattered the light.

"Will you marry me, Betsy? Will you share your life and your heart with me?"

She leaned over and cupped his face in her hands and gently kissed his lips. "Yes."

He slipped the ring on her finger and suddenly she was in his arms. Tears of happiness welled up and overflowed. As if on cue, Puffy jumped high in the air, barking and trying to kiss them both.

Moments later, dazed and breathing hard, Betsy stepped back from his embrace, lifting her hand to gaze at the brilliant stone. Its brightness was only surpassed by the love she had for the man who'd given it to her.

"You and no other," she murmured.

"Forever," he vowed.

"Forever," she repeated, ready to embrace the future with the man she loved, knowing there wasn't anything they couldn't face...together.

EPILOGUE

"I never thought it was possible to pull together a wedding in six weeks," Betsy gazed up at her husband of seven hours then around the crowded ballroom.

The fact that the Spring Gulch Country Club was still decorated for Valentine's Day seemed appropriate because her wedding day three days after had been filled with passion. The promise of her and Ryan's love had been fulfilled when they'd said their vows this afternoon in a small ceremony in the mountains. Betsy smiled. "I can't believe so many people showed up."

"They wouldn't have missed it." Ryan's hand rested on her waist. "Just like the preliminary hearing. They make time for what's important."

When Betsy had arrived at the courthouse last month, she'd been stunned to find the place packed. Their friends had all turned out to show their support.

Chad and his attorney had been shocked. At first Betsy thought he might waive the prelim, but both Betsy and the woman he'd violated had been allowed to testify. Despite the stress, Betsy had achieved a measure of peace by confronting her attacker in court.

When Chad's attorney had tried to bring Ryan into the picture, Betsy hadn't gotten defensive. She'd simply stuck to the facts and reiterated that anything that had gone on between her and her fiancé had been consensual.

Though nothing had been decided, rumors around town were that Chad's attorney was proposing a plea agreement. That part of Betsy's life would soon be relegated to the past. But Betsy had already decided that once they got back from the honeymoon, she was going to get involved with the Teton County Victim Services.

"You look a million miles away." Her husband leaned over, brushing his lips against her hair.

Betsy leaned into his embrace, resting her head against his shoulder. "I feel so blessed."

Puffy sat with a group of children, a shimmery white bow askew about her neck. The Pomeranian had been the consummate ring bearer, prancing down the red carpet of the small church.

Mr. Marstand, looking resplendent in the tux he'd worn when he'd walked Betsy down the aisle, was dancing with one of Aunt Agatha's bridge partners.

Scattered around the large room were friends and their families laughing, talking and dancing. Her gaze settled on Cole and Meg Lassiter's son, Charlie. Meg had mentioned that last year the little boy had been involved in "Mutton Busting" at the Little Buckeroo Rodeo in Pinedale.

Would Ryan want his son or daughter to be involved in rodeo activities? Betsy was curious, but not concerned. She knew when the time came that she and Ryan would make that decision together.

"If you're worried about the Love Token," Ryan said in a low tone, "I'm confident it will show up."

The day after he'd asked her to marry him, the medallion had gone missing. Again.

Ryan chuckled and added. "It'll probably show up before some big occasion, like when we find out we're pregnant."

Betsy thought about the test she'd taken just that morning. Her lips curved upward.

"I can't believe it," Ryan said. "There it is."

"Where?"

"Stuck to the side of the cake." His voice was filled with disbelief. "How the heck did it get *there?*"

Betsy wound her arms around his neck. "You're so smart."

Ryan tilted his head. "Because I predicted that it would show up and it did?"

"Because—" She pressed a kiss against the edge of his lips. "You said it would show up when we find out we're pregnant."

"When we—" He froze. "Are you saying what I think you're saying?"

Betsy nodded. Her smile widened. "I did the test this morning. It was positive."

Ryan let out a whoop and spun her around until they were both laughing and out of breath. As his lips closed over hers, Princess Betsy realized that life didn't get much better than life with Prince Ryan in the Kingdom of Jackson Hole.

I really enjoyed writing His Hometown Girl. Ryan and Betsy are simply a perfect match. When you toss Puffy into the mix, they're already a happy family of three!

If you love uplifting romance, like His Hometown Girl, you're going to LOVE Second Chance Family. I'll let you in on a little secret. There's an interesting twist that I don't think you'll see coming.

Put up your feet, grab your Kindle and start enjoying Second Chance Family now!

Or keeping reading for a sneak peek.

SNEAK PEEK OF SECOND CHANCE FAMILY

Chapter One

Margaret Fisher glanced around the attorney's waiting room, her heart fluttering like a hummingbird on steroids. Too nervous to concentrate on the magazine in her lap, she took a couple of deep breaths and let her gaze linger on her surroundings.

The random-width plank floor made from exotic woods added visual appeal while the muted tan-colored walls provided the perfect foil for the "artwork" in the room. Like many businesses in Jackson Hole, the designer had carried the cowboy theme a bit too far for her liking. Ryan Harcourt's rodeo awards were featured prominently on the wall and a well-oiled saddle sat on display in one corner.

Despite Ryan having graduated from a prestigious east coast law school, there was not a diploma in sight. Margaret assumed there would be one in his office. It didn't surprise her to see him focus on his roots in the outer waiting area. In Jackson Hole, the majority of his clients would relate better to his rodeo background than to his Ivy League education.

The young attorney—and former champion bull rider—was

well-known to Margaret. He'd been a classmate of hers at Jackson Hole High School as well as a close friend of Margaret's boyfriend, Cole Lassiter. Not boyfriend, she corrected herself. Cole was simply the jerk who acted as if he loved her, took her virginity and then unceremoniously dumped her, all without taking her on a single date.

It had been years since she'd seen Cole. She'd half expected their paths to cross at the funeral. After all, growing up, he and Janae had been next-door neighbors. Margaret had also heard he stopped in to see Janae and Ty whenever he was in town. But then, Cole hadn't bothered to come to her parents' funeral so it hadn't surprised her when he didn't show. Respect didn't seem to be a word in his vocabulary.

"Charlie, would you like to play with these?" Lexi Delacourt, the social worker seated to Margaret's right, opened the large colorful bag and let the child she'd brought with her peer inside.

Margaret smiled as the boy's eyes brightened, and she pushed aside the old memories. There were more important things to think about today. Cole was the past. Today was about her future. Just like it had been when she'd sat in the attorney's office on her seventeenth birthday. That day she'd been with her seven siblings. The normal laughter and joking that always occurred when they were all in the same room had been noticeably absent.

It was understandable, of course. They'd been stressed and grieving. Anxious about what was going to happen to them now that their parents had died. She wondered if Charlie had that same sick feeling in the pit of his stomach she'd had back then.

She cast a sideways glance at the little boy who was now lining up plastic dinosaurs on the rough-hewn top of the wooden trunk coffee table. The six-year-old was the son of Margaret's childhood friend, Janae, and her husband, Ty.

Now they were both gone, killed in an accident only weeks before Christmas near Brown's Curve on Route 22. The same stretch of Jackson Hole roadway where her folks had died.

It's not fair.

Tears stung the back of Margaret's eyes. Though she hadn't seen as much of her friend as she'd have liked since leaving Wyoming fifteen years ago, thanks to the internet and cell phones, she and Janae had remained close confidantes and friends.

Without warning, Charlie jumped up from the brown-and-white cowhide sofa, his boots making a loud thud on the floor.

"I'm gonna look at the fish," he announced to Lexi when she cast him a questioning look.

He crossed the room looking adorable in his blue chambray shirt, jeans and cowboy boots. He'd been wearing something similar in the picture Janae had emailed Margaret last summer, the one taken at the Lil' Buckeroo Rodeo in Pinedale.

Charlie had been a much-loved child. Her friend had embraced motherhood and Ty had doted on his son. Both wanted more children, but for some reason Janae had been unable to get pregnant again. They'd been trying since Charlie turned two and this past year had started expensive fertility treatments.

Margaret could understand why her friends had wanted more children. She'd fallen under Charlie's sweet spell when she'd returned to Jackson Hole last Christmas for the christening of her brother's twin babies. She'd been thrilled for Travis and at the same time envious of the way his life had so happily fallen into place. Before leaving town she'd stopped and spent time with Janae and her family.

When it came time for her to leave, Charlie had wrapped his arms around her and given her a kiss. Looping an arm around his waist, Margaret had teased Janae that she was taking him with her. But, as always, she'd left Wyoming alone, single seat on the aisle.

"They're ginormous." Charlie whirled around, his eyes wide with awe.

"Super big," Margaret agreed then sighed when he turned back to the aquarium. She'd once hoped to have a husband to love and a child like Charlie to cherish. But she was already in her early thirties and that dream was looking less likely with each passing year.

As a physical therapist who dealt primarily with stroke patients, Margaret didn't have much opportunity to meet eligible men at work. And she'd never been one for the bar scene. To complicate matters, most of her friends were married. Of course, she reminded herself, if she'd been willing to exchange vows with a man she liked and respected but wasn't madly in love with, she'd be married, too.

But last year, after much soul-searching, she broke it off with her fiancé. She hadn't regretted her decision. Okay, maybe a couple of times on dark, lonely nights when she remembered how good he'd been to her and feared she'd simply been expecting too much. After all, they'd gotten along well and had fun when they were together. Did "madly in love" really have to be part of the equation?

She'd wondered.

Then she'd run into him and his new girlfriend a couple of weeks ago. The way they looked at each other told her she'd been right to call off the wedding. Not only for her sake but for his. Everyone deserved to be loved with such passion.

"Me an' my dad used to go fishing," Charlie said, gazing at the tank. "Mommy would sometimes come, too. But Daddy had to put the worm on the hook for her."

"That was nice of him." Lexi said. "You had a nice daddy."

Having Lexi overseeing Charlie's case felt almost like having a family member involved. When the attractive social worker with the sleek brown bob had introduced herself, she'd mentioned she was a good friend of Margaret's older brother, Travis, a local ob-gyn.

Margaret knew Travis and his wife, Mary Karen, had a group

of close-knit friends. Like Lexi, all were married with children. Margaret sighed. Sometimes it felt as if everyone had the life she wanted...except her.

"Have you seen the will?" Lexi asked in a low tone, leaning over the arm of her chair.

Margaret shook her head. "But I have a good idea what's in it."

At the funeral, when Ryan asked her to come to his office for the reading, she hadn't been surprised by the request. Last year, when one of their high school classmates had died of cancer, Janae had broached the subject of Margaret raising Charlie if anything should happen to her and Ty. She'd been flattered but wondered why Janae wouldn't want her child raised by family.

Janae had informed her she'd already approached her parents. Apparently they'd stammered and offered a whole litany of excuses—they'd retired to Florida because of Larry's health, the gated community they'd settled into didn't allow children, it would be best for Charlie to remain in familiar surroundings....

Margaret's heart had ached for her friend. All these years Janae had been right. She'd always insisted that her parents really had only one child—her brother—and that she wasn't that important to them.

Ty's own family situation wasn't much better. He'd been estranged from them for years. They'd sent a small plant for the memorial service.

"Charlie, honey, don't press so hard against the glass," Lexi called out to the boy but made no move to get up.

With an older child and a busy toddler at home, this was probably the only chance the social worker had to rest. Margaret stifled a smile and rose to her feet. She crossed the room, her heels clicking loudly on the hardwood. Normally she favored more comfortable clothing than the silver-blue suit and certainly more sensible footwear than high heels. But this had seemed an appropriate day to forgo comfort for something more stylish and businesslike.

She crouched down beside the boy, who had his nose pressed against the aquarium glass. "Which one do you like best?"

"The yellow one." Charlie pointed to a large silver angelfish with a blanket of gold over the head and back.

"It's very pretty." Margaret resisted the urge to brush the tousle of chocolate-brown hair back from his face. "Do you remember me, Charlie? I'm Margaret. I was a friend of your mom."

The boy turned to face her, his eyes a deep, dark blue. "Pastor says my mommy and daddy are with Jesus in heaven."

Margaret took a deep breath and blinked back tears. The sermon at the funeral had been comforting, but it was still hard to accept that it had been her childhood friend lying in one of the two caskets at the front of the church. Heartbreaking to realize she and Janae would never laugh over the phone or Tweet pithy one-liners to each other.

Still, she believed the pastor when he'd said Janae and Ty were in a better place. Her friend had such a quirky sense of humor that Margaret had no doubt at this very moment she was livening up the heavenly throng with Ty cheering her on.

"Do you think they're coming back for me?" he asked in a small voice.

"I'm afraid not," Margaret said softly. She cursed her honesty when his eyes filled with tears and his bottom lip began to tremble. "But I know they're still watching over you. And that they love you very much."

"I want my mommy." The boy's arms stiffened at his sides and his hands clenched into tiny fists. "Bring her here. Now."

Her heart rose to her throat. *If only I could bring her back. And Ty, too.*

Like a whirlwind sweeping across the plains, as quickly as Charlie's anger flared, it disappeared and he began to cry.

Margaret wrapped her arms around him, murmuring soothing words and holding him tight. After several heartbeats he quit struggling. After several more she felt him relax in her arms.

From her own experience, she knew a little about what he'd be going through in the weeks and months ahead. She vowed to make this transition as easy as possible for him.

With his soft curls still pressed against her cheek, Margaret heard the attorney's office door open. But she couldn't move a muscle. The child had his arms around her, holding her as tight as a drowning sailor would grasp a life preserver.

"Margaret." Ryan moved to her side and placed a hand on her shoulder. "Lexi will take good care of him while we talk."

"Charlie, I have something really cool to show you." The social worker peeled the boy from Margaret's arms. "The office down the hall has several gigantic fish."

"Bigger than those?" Charlie pointed to the aquarium, his tears like little crystals on his long lashes.

"Oh, my goodness, yes. Way bigger." Lexi held out her hand. "Come with me and we'll go see them."

The little boy hesitated, glancing at Margaret.

"I'm not going anywhere," Margaret assured him. "I'll be here when you get back."

After a long moment, Charlie put his fingers in the social worker's hand. "I wanna see the fishes."

Lexi smiled at Margaret and gave the attorney a wink. "We won't be long."

Margaret watched them leave. Her heart warmed when Charlie returned her wave.

"I'm glad you could make it." Ryan gestured toward his office then stepped aside to let her pass. "We're waiting for one more but there's some preliminary stuff we can get started on."

Margaret smiled, finding it strangely refreshing to hear an attorney use the word stuff. She took a seat in front of his desk, wondering who it was Ryan was expecting. It hadn't crossed her mind that anyone else would show up for the reading. "Did Janae's parents change their minds and decide to stay in town a little while longer?"

"Nothing like that." The attorney took a seat in the cowhide-and-leather swivel desk chair and offered her an easy smile.

Despite being thrown to the ground and stomped on by bulls weighing close to two thousand pounds, Ryan looked no worse for wear. His face was unscarred and his hair as dark and thick as it had been in school. He was a cute guy but Ryan had never made her heart skip a beat.

Back then, people who didn't know him well had always confused him with Cole. Both had dark hair and slender, athletic builds. But Ryan's eyes were a silvery-gray while Cole's eyes were as blue as the ocean.

In her young, stupid days, Margaret had been convinced she could drown in Cole's eyes. She resisted the urge to gag.

Ryan shifted in his seat and glanced at his watch. Tiny lines furrowed his brow.

If Margaret didn't know better, she'd say he was worried. But that didn't make sense. What did he have to be concerned about? Unless he thought she was having second thoughts about raising Charlie. Could he be afraid she was going to bail on the boy?

Margaret leaned forward and rested both hands on the edge of the desk. "Janae and I talked last year about her and Ty's wishes, should anything happen to them. I'm fully aware she wanted me to—"

The outer office door jingled.

Ryan's head jerked toward the sound.

Margaret paused and sat back.

Before she could say another word, Ryan leaped from his seat and rounded the desk. "I'll get it."

But he didn't have time to reach the door before it swung open. Turning in her seat to gawk at the new arrival seemed a little gauche, so Margaret waited for the visitor to stroll into view.

"It's good to see you," Ryan said.

"I hope I didn't keep you waiting long."

Margaret froze. The man's voice sounded all too familiar. She shivered as the sexy voice continued. "DFW got snowed in and all the flights backed up."

She didn't need to turn in her chair to know who Ryan had so warmly welcomed. Even after all these years, she recognized his voice. It was the same sexy rumble that had whispered sweet nothings in her ear when she'd been sixteen. The same husky voice that had shook with emotion when he'd pronounced her his sweetheart and given her a silver heart-shaped locket for Valentine's Day. The same voice that she hadn't heard again after they'd made love in the backseat of his old Chevy.

She dug her nails into her palms.

"You're lucky you didn't make it in yesterday morning. We had a jet go off the runway," Ryan rattled on. "Typical November weather."

"Anyone who grew up in this region should know better than to fly in the day of any event, especially at this time of year." Margaret turned in her seat, unable to sit still a moment longer. "Unless it was your intent all along to miss the funeral."

She had only a second to brace herself before Cole fixed his brilliant blue eyes on her, and to be startled at the sight of him on crutches.

"You remember Margaret Fisher." Ryan gestured to her with a broad sweep of a hand. "She went to high school with us."

It didn't surprise Margaret that Ryan would feel the need to clarify. After all, it wasn't as if they'd run in the same social circle back then. Ryan and Cole had been popular, while she'd been studious, shy and completely forgettable. A part of her had wondered if he'd ever mentioned his involvement with her to his friends. Apparently not.

Cole's expression gave nothing away. "Of course, I remember Meg."

"Meg?" Ryan lifted a brow. "I don't know that I've ever heard anyone call her that before."

That's because no one else ever had, only Cole.

"I meant, Margaret," Cole returned easily.

Ryan's eyes held a curious gleam and Margaret got the feeling he knew there was more to the story than a simple verbal faux pas.

"You're looking well," Cole said to her when the silence lengthened.

Other than the crutches and the brace on his right knee, she supposed she could say the same about him. His hair was a little longer now, brushing his collar in a stylish cut. The hand-tailored dark suit he wore emphasized broad shoulders and lean hips. Surprisingly, he'd foregone a tie and left his gray shirt unbuttoned at the neck.

While she grudgingly admitted he looked...attractive...she had no use for him or for the words that came so easy to his tongue. Margaret lifted her chin. "Your friend appears to be too much of a gentleman to tell you—but this is a private business meeting."

She could have cheered when her tone came out cool with just the slightest amount of indifference.

Cole's brows pulled together and he shot Ryan a puzzled glance. "You told me this was the time you'd set aside to go over Ty and Janae's will."

Margaret narrowed her gaze and focused on Cole. "You must really be doing badly if you came all this way just to see if they left you anything."

For a second she regretted speaking so frankly. Being brash wasn't her style. Then she recalled how Cole had treated her and she decided she was being too kind.

"I'm doing quite well, not that it's any of your concern."

Cole's expression darkened. He turned to Ryan. "What the hell is going on here?"

A look of guilt crossed the attorney's face and the gaze he shot her was filled with apology.

Margaret had always been intuitive. The unique gift that had failed her only once before was now telling her that something was about to go wrong. Dreadfully wrong.

"Ryan?" Margaret choked out the attorney's name, finding breathing suddenly difficult.

"Neither of you have the complete picture, not yet." Ryan gestured for Cole to take a seat then exhaled a harsh breath. "That's the way Ty and Janae wanted it."

Then this wasn't a chance meeting, but something orchestrated from the grave by Margaret's oldest and dearest friend. Oh, Janae, what have you done?

"I think I'd better sit down." With lips pressed tightly together, Cole moved carefully across the slippery wood floor and eased himself into the only empty chair in the room, the one next to hers.

Though a big part of her life revolved around physical rehabilitation, she didn't comment on his unsteady gait or ask about his injury. Quite simply she didn't care. She couldn't care. Not about him. Or his gimpy leg.

The only thing she wanted to know was why he was at this meeting…and how soon he'd be leaving.

Grab your copy and get swept up in a heartwarming story guaranteed to uplift and delight you!

ALSO BY CINDY KIRK

Good Hope Series

The Good Hope series is a must-read for those who love stories that uplift and bring a smile to your face.

GraceTown Series

Enchanting stories that are a perfect mixture of romance, friendship, and magical moments set in a community known for unexplainable happenings.

Hazel Green Series

These heartwarming stories, set in the tight-knit community of Hazel Green, are sure to move you, uplift you, inspire and delight you. Enjoy uplifting romances that will keep you turning the page!

Holly Pointe Series

Readers say "If you are looking for a festive, romantic read this Christmas, these are the books for you."

Jackson Hole Series

Heartwarming and uplifting stories set in beautiful Jackson Hole, Wyoming.

Silver Creek Series

Engaging and heartfelt romances centered around two powerful families whose fortunes were forged in the Colorado silver mines.

Sweet River Montana Series

A community serving up a slice of small-town Montana life, where helping hands abound and people fall in love in the context of home and family.

Made in the USA
Columbia, SC
01 December 2022

72479560R00129